"I only noticed because I can't seem to take my eyes off you whenever you're around."

And there it was. The acknowledgement of whatever this was. Attraction. Curiosity. Carnality.

"I thought we weren't going to do this," she said softly. She kept her hands folded tightly in her lap to keep them from going where they wanted to go—on him. "I'm only here for a few days."

"Then there's no danger. We both know what's what. We're going in with our eyes wide open."

"Are you seducing me, Rhys?" His thumb toyed with her lower lip and her eyes drifted closed.

"With any luck." He moved closer, leaning forward slightly so she began to recline against the cushions. "We're adults," he stated. "We're both wondering. It doesn't have to go any deeper than that."

Tentatively she lifted her hand and touched his face. "Usually I'm the confident one who goes after what she wants."

He smiled a little, his gaze dropping to her lips. "You don't want this? I could have sworn you did."

"I didn't say that…" she whispered, sliding deeper into the cushions.

"That's what I thought."

His voice was husky now, shivering along her nerve-endings. He leaned closer until he was less than a breath away.

Dear Reader

There's something extra special about a Christmas wedding. Red satin dresses, poinsettias, candlelight... It's gorgeous and romantic, and when I began writing this book I knew I wanted Taylor Shepard to be planning this event for her brother Callum and his bride Avery, from LITTLE COWGIRL ON HIS DOORSTEP.

Of course planning a wedding during the Christmas season can also be very stressful. And when you're a bit of a perfectionist who's working on a tight timeline it's even more so. So the last thing Taylor needs is an opinionated groomsman who seems to get under her skin far too easily. Rhys Bullock is a man who is steady as an oak and a bit too small-town for Taylor. Until she gets to know him better and realises he's a little more complicated than he seems on the outside. Not to mention the inexplicable chemistry they seem to have together...

This book is the first in a duet about the Shepard siblings, Taylor and Jack. It was great fun to write, and is my last book for the Mills & Boon® Romance line, although you can find my future books as eBooks in Mills & Boon American Romance®.

Thank you for being so wonderful during my years with Mills & Boon® Romance, and I hope to see you often in the future!

With my very best wishes

Donna

A CADENCE CREEK CHRISTMAS

BY
DONNA ALWARD

MILLS
BOON

First published in Great Britain 2013
by Mills & Boon, an imprint of Harlequin (UK) Limited.
Harlequin (UK) Limited, Eton House, 18-24 Paradise Road,
Richmond, Surrey TW9 1SR

© Donna Alward 2013

ISBN: 978 0 263 23583 8

Harlequin (UK) policy is to use papers that are natural, renewable and recyclable products and made from wood grown in sustainable forests. The logging and manufacturing process conform to the legal environmental regulations of the country of origin.

Printed and bound in Great Britain
by CPI Antony Rowe, Chippenham, Wiltshire

A busy wife and mother of three (two daughters and the family dog), **Donna Alward** believes hers is the best job in the world: a combination of stay-at-home mum and romance novelist. An avid reader since childhood, Donna always made up her own stories. She completed her arts degree in English literature in 1994, but it wasn't until 2001 that she penned her first full-length novel and found herself hooked on writing romance. In 2006 she sold her first manuscript, and now writes warm, emotional stories for Mills & Boon®.

In her new home office in Nova Scotia, Donna loves being back on the east coast of Canada after nearly twelve years in Alberta, where her career began, writing about cowboys and the West. Donna's debut romance, HIRED BY THE COWBOY, was awarded the Bookseller's Best Award in 2008 for Best Traditional Romance.

With the Atlantic Ocean only minutes from her doorstep, Donna has found a fresh take on life and promises even more great romances in the near future!

Donna loves to hear from readers. You can contact her through her website, www.donnaalward.com, her page at www.myspace.com/dalward, or through her publisher.

Books by Donna Alward:

A COWBOY TO COME HOME TO
LITTLE COWGIRL ON HIS DOORSTEP
THE REBEL RANCHER
THE LAST REAL COWBOY
HOW A COWBOY STOLE HER HEART
A FAMILY FOR THE RUGGED RANCHER
HONEYMOON WITH THE RANCHER

Did you know these are also available as eBooks?
Visit www.millsandboon.co.uk

To the Mills & Boon® Romance authors—
my writing family.
You guys are the best.

CHAPTER ONE

TAYLOR SHEPARD FROWNED as she assessed the lineup of men before her. All five of them were big, burly and, with the exception of her brother Jack, looked irritated beyond belief.

"Come on, Taylor, can't we take these monkey suits off?"

Her oldest brother, Callum, pleaded with her. Along with his best man and groomsmen, he'd spent the past half hour trying on various tuxedo styles. Callum, being her brother and, of course, the groom, was the spokesman for the lot.

"If you want to show up at your wedding in jeans and boots, be my guest. I don't think your bride would appreciate that too much, though."

A muffled snort came from down the line. Her head snapped toward the sound and she saw one of the groomsmen—Rhys, if she remembered correctly—struggling to keep a straight face.

"Keep it up," she warned severely, "and you'll be the one trying on a cravat."

His face sobered in an instant.

"This was supposed to be a small and simple wedding," Callum reminded her. "Not one of your massive events."

"And it will be. But small and simple doesn't mean it

can't be classy." She pinned him with a stare. "Your soon-to-be wife trusts me. Besides, you need to balance your look with the wedding dress and flower girl dress for Nell." She paused and played her trump card. "They're going to be *beautiful*."

There'd be little argument out of Callum now. All it took was the mention of Avery and his baby daughter and the tough ex-soldier turned into a marshmallow. She thought it was fantastic. He'd needed someone like Avery for a long time. Not to mention how fatherhood had changed him. He had the family he'd always wanted.

She examined each man carefully. "I don't like the red vests," she decreed. She went up to Sam Diamond and tugged on the lapels of his jacket. "And not double-breasted. The green vests, like Tyson's here. The single-breasted jacket like Jack has on, which is much simpler." She smiled up at her brother, easily the most comfortable man in the group. Jack wouldn't give her a moment's trouble, not about this anyway. She got to the last body in the line and looked up.

Dark eyes looked down into hers. A little serious, a little bit of put-upon patience, and a surprising warmth that made her think he had a good sense of humor. She reached up and gave his tie a tug, straightening it. "And not the bolo tie, either. The crossover that Rhys is wearing is classier and still very Western."

Her fingertips grazed the starchy fabric of his shirt as she dropped her hand. It was a negligible touch, barely worth noticing, except the slight contact made something interesting tumble around in her stomach. Her gaze darted up to his again and discovered he was watching her steadily in a way that made her feel both excited and awkward.

Interesting. Because in her line of work she dealt with

all sorts of men every day. Rich men, powerful men, men who liked other men and men who couldn't keep their hands to themselves. She knew how to handle herself. Was never tempted to flirt unless it was a business strategy. She was very good at reading people, figuring out their tastes and wants and knowing what methods she needed to use to deliver them.

So getting a fluttery feeling from barely touching Rhys Bullock was a surprise indeed. And feeling awkward? Well, that was practically unheard of. Of course, it could be that she was just very out of practice. She'd been far too busy building her business to do much dating.

She straightened her shoulders and took a step backward. "Okay, now on to footwear."

Groans went up the line.

She smiled. "Guys, really. This will be the best part. I was thinking black boots which we can get wherever you prefer to buy your boots. No patent dress shoes. Put on the boots you wore here so we can accurately measure your inseam for length. Then we'll finish up your measurements and you're done." She made a dismissive sound. "Honestly, what a bunch of babies."

She was having fun now, teasing the guys. They were good men but not much for dressing up. She got that. Their standard uniform was jeans and boots, plaid shirts and Stetsons. Tuxedo fittings had to be torture.

Still, it didn't matter if this was her brother's wedding or a client's A-list party. Or if she was being paid or doing it as a wedding gift. Avery and Callum's day would be exactly what it should be because she'd oversee every last detail.

And if she were being honest with herself, it was a relief to get out of Vancouver for a while and deal with "real" people. It had been exhausting lately. Most of her clients were rich and used to getting exactly what they wanted exactly when they wanted it. Their sense of entitlement could be a bit much. Not to mention the unorthodox requests. She sometimes wondered what sort of reality these people lived in.

As she looked after the ordering details, one of the alterations staff did measurements. Another half hour and they were all done and standing out in the sunshine again. Taylor pulled out her phone and scanned her to-do list for today. She had to drive back to Cadence Creek and meet with Melissa Stone, the florist at Foothills Floral. The final order was going to be placed today—after all, the wedding was less than two weeks away now. All this should have been done a month ago or even more, but Taylor knew there were ways to get things done in a hurry if needs be. Like with the tuxes and invitations. Both should have been tended to months ago but it had merely taken a few phone calls and it had all been sorted. A little out of Callum's budget, perhaps, but he didn't need to know that. She was good for it. *Exclusive!*—her event planning business—had treated her well the past few years.

Still, there was no time to waste. She closed her calendar and looked up.

The group of them were standing around chatting, something about a lodge north of town and what had happened to the rancher who'd owned it. Jack was listening intently, but Rhys was missing. Had he left already?

The bell on the door chimed behind her, and she turned to see Rhys walking through. He looked far more himself now in black jeans and a black, tan and red plaid shirt beneath a sheepskin jacket. His boots were brown and weathered and as he stepped on to the sidewalk he dipped his head just a little and placed a well-worn hat on top. Taylor half smiled. The hat looked like an old friend; shaped precisely to his head, worn-in and comfortable.

"Feel better?" she asked, smiling.

"I'm not much for dressing up," he replied simply.

"I know. None of you are, really. But it's only for one day. You're all going to look very handsome."

"Is that so?"

Her cheeks heated a little. Rhys's best feature was his eyes. And he was tall and well-built, just the way she liked her men. Perhaps it was growing up the way she had. They'd all been outdoor kids. Heck, Callum had joined the military and Jack had been a pro downhill skier until he'd blown his knee out at Val d'Isère.

But Rhys wasn't classically handsome. Not in the way that Tyson Diamond was, for instance. In this group Rhys would be the one who would probably be overlooked. His cheekbones were high and defined and his jawbone unrelenting, giving him a rough appearance. His lips looked well-shaped but it was hard to tell—the closest she'd seen him come to smiling was the clandestine chuckle while they were inside.

But it was the way he'd answered that piqued her interest. *Is that so?* he'd asked, as if he couldn't care one way or the other if anyone thought him handsome or not.

It was quite refreshing.

"I should get going," she said, lifting her chin. "I've got to be back to town in thirty minutes for another appointment. Thanks for coming out. It'll be easy for you from here on in. Weddings do tend to be mostly women's business." At least with these sorts of men…

"Drive carefully then," he said, tipping his hat. "No sense rushing. The creek isn't going anywhere."

"Thanks, but I'd like to be on time just the same." She gave him a brief nod and turned to the assembled group.

"I've got to go. Thanks everyone." She put her hand on Callum's shoulder and went up on tiptoe to kiss his cheek. "See you soon." She did the same for Jack. "When are you flying out?"

He shrugged. "I'm going to hang around for a few days. I've got to be back in Montana for meetings on Monday, though, and then I'm flying in the Thursday before the wedding."

"Let's have lunch before you go back."

"You got it. Text me."

With a quick wave Taylor hurried across the parking lot, her heeled boots echoing on the pavement. She turned the car heater on high and rubbed her hands together— December in Alberta was colder than on the coast and she felt chilled to the bone all the time.

She was down to twenty-five minutes. As a light snow began to fall, she put her rental car in gear and pulled out, checking her GPS for the quickest route to the highway.

Three weeks. That was how long she had to decompress. She'd take care of Callum's wedding and then enjoy one indulgent week of vacation before heading home and working on the final preparations for New Year's. This year's planning involved taking over an entire warehouse and transforming it into an under the sea kingdom.

It all seemed quite ridiculous. And because it did, she knew that it was time she took a vacation. Even one as short as a week in some small, backwater Alberta town. Thank goodness her assistant, Alicia, was completely capable and could handle things in Taylor's absence.

She turned on the wipers and sighed. Compared to the crazy demands of her normal events, she knew she could do this wedding with her eyes closed.

If that were true, though, why was she having so much fun and dreading going back to Vancouver so very much?

* * *

It was already dark when Taylor whipped out her phone, brought up her to-do list and started punching in brief notes with her thumbs. Her fingers were numb with cold and she'd been out of the flower shop for a whole minute and a half. Where on earth was the frigid air coming from anyway? Shivering and walking toward the town's B&B, she hurriedly typed in one last detail she didn't want to forget. Instead of typing the word "cedar," however, she felt a sharp pain in her shoulder as she bounced off something very big and hard.

"Hey," she growled. "Watch where you're going!"

She looked up to find Rhys Bullock staring down at her, a scowl marking his angular face.

"Oh, it's you," she said, letting out a puff of annoyance.

He knelt down and retrieved her phone, stood up and handed it over. "Hope it didn't break," he said. His tone suggested that he wasn't quite sincere in that sentiment.

"The rubber cover is supposed to protect it. It'll be fine."

"Maybe next time you should watch where you're going. Stop and sit down before you start typing."

"It's too damn cold to stop," she grumbled.

He laughed then, the expulsion of breath forming a white cloud around his head. "Not used to an arctic front? This isn't cold. Wait until it's minus forty."

"Not a chance."

"That's right. You're only here for the wedding."

"If you'll excuse me, I'd like to get out of the cold before my fingertips fall off." She tried to ignore how his face changed when he laughed, softening the severe lines. A smattering of tiny marks added character to his tanned skin. If she had to come up with one word to describe Rhys, it would be *weathered*. It wasn't necessarily a bad thing.

He took a step closer and to her surprise reached into her pocket and took out her gloves. Then he took the phone from her hands, dropped it in the pocket and handed over the gloves. "This will help."

She raised an eyebrow. "That was presumptuous of you."

He shrugged. "Ms. Shepard, I'm pretty much used to keeping things simple and doing what has to be done. If your fingers are cold, put on your gloves."

She shoved her fingers into the fuzzy warmth, her temper simmering. He spoke to her as if she were a child!

"Now," he said calmly, "where are you headed? It's dark. I'll walk you."

Her temper disintegrated under the weight of her disbelief. She laughed. "Are you serious? This is Cadence Creek. I think I'll be safe walking two blocks to my accommodations." Good Lord. She lived in one of the largest cities in Canada. She knew how to look out for herself!

"Maybe I just want to make sure you don't start texting and walk out into traffic," he suggested. "You must be going to Jim's then." He named the bed and breakfast owner.

"That's right."

He turned around so they were facing the same direction. "Let's go," he suggested.

She fell into step because she didn't know what else to do. He seemed rather determined and it would take all of five minutes to walk to the rambling house that provided the town's only accommodation. To her mind the dive motel out on the highway didn't count. She watched as he tipped his hat to an older lady coming out of the drugstore and then gave a nod to a few men standing on the steps of the hardware. He might be gruff and bossy and not all that pretty to look at, but she had to give Rhys one thing—his manners were impeccable.

The light dusting of snow earlier covered the sidewalk and even grouchy Taylor had to admit that it was pretty, especially in the dark with the town's Christmas lights casting colored shadows on its surface. Each old-fashioned lamppost held a pine wreath with a red bow. Storefronts were decorated with garland on their railings and twinkle lights. Christmas trees peeked through front windows and jolly Santas and snowmen grinned from front yards.

Cadence Creek at the holidays was like one of those Christmas card towns that Taylor hadn't believed truly existed. Being here wasn't really so bad. Even if it was a little…boring.

They stopped at a crosswalk. And as they did her stomach gave out a long, loud rumble.

Rhys put his hand at her elbow and they stepped off the curb. But instead of going right on the other side, he guided her to the left.

"Um, the B&B is that way," she said, turning her head and pointing in the opposite direction.

"When did you eat last?" he asked.

She fought the urge to sigh. "None of your business."

Undeterred, he kept walking and kept the pressure at her elbow. "Jim and Kathleen don't provide dinner. You need something to eat."

She stopped dead in her tracks. Rhys carried on for a few steps until he realized she wasn't with him then he stopped and turned around. "What?"

"How old am I?"

His brows wrinkled, forming a crease above his nose. "How could I possibly know that?"

"Do I look like an adult to you?"

Something flared in his eyes as his gaze slid from her face down to her boots and back up again. "Yes'm."

She swallowed. "You can't herd me like you herd your cattle, Mr. Bullock."

"I don't herd cattle," he responded.

"You don't?"

"No ma'am. I work with the horses. Especially the skittish ones."

"Well, then," she floundered and then recovered, ignoring that a snowflake had just fallen and landed on the tip of her nose. "I'm not one of your horses. You can't make me eat just because you say so."

He shrugged. "Can't make the horses do that, either. Trick is to make them *want* to do what I want." He gave her a level stare. "I'm pretty good at that."

"Your ego isn't suffering, I see."

His lips twitched. "No, ma'am. Everyone has a skill. Smart man knows what his is, that's all."

God, she didn't want to be amused. He was a bull-headed, overbearing macho cowboy type who probably called women "little lady" and thought he was all that. But she was amused and to be honest she'd enjoyed sparring with him just a little bit. At least he wasn't a pampered brat like most people she met.

She let out the tension in her shoulders. "Where are you taking me, then?" She'd seriously considered ordering a pizza and having it delivered to the B&B. It wasn't like there was a plethora of dining choices in Cadence Creek.

"Just to the Wagon Wheel. Best food in town."

"I've been. I had lunch there yesterday." And breakfast in the dining room of the bed and breakfast and then dinner was a fast-food burger grabbed on the way back from the stationery supply store in Edmonton.

The lunch had definitely been the best meal—home-made chicken soup, thick with big chunks of chicken, veg-etables and the temptation of a warm roll which she'd left behind, not wanting the extra carbs.

Her stomach growled again, probably from the mere thought of the food at the diner.

"Fine. I'll go get some takeout. Will that make you happy?"

He shrugged. "It's not about me. But now that you men-tion it, I think tonight is pot roast. I could do with some of that myself." He turned and started walking away.

Reluctantly she followed a step behind him. At least he didn't have that darned proprietary hand under her elbow anymore. Half a block away she could smell the food. The aroma of the standard fare—fries and the like—hit first, but then the undertones touched her nostrils: beef, bread and baking.

Her mouth watered as she reminded herself that she had a bridesmaid's dress to fit into as well. Pot roast would be good. But she would absolutely say no to dessert.

It was warm inside the diner. The blast of heat was a glorious welcome and the scents that were hinted at out-side filled the air inside. Christmas music played from an ancient jukebox in the corner. The whole place was deco-rated for the holidays, but in the evening with everything lit up it looked very different than it had yesterday at noon. Mini-lights ran the length of the lunch counter and the tree in a back corner had flashing lights and a star topper that pulsed like a camera flash. The prevalence of vinyl and chrome made her feel like she was in a time warp.

Two-thirds of the tables were filled with people, all talking animatedly over the music. Rhys gave a wave to a group in a corner and then, to her surprise, slipped be-hind the cash register and went straight into the kitchen.

Through the order window she saw him grin at an older

woman in a huge cobbler's apron who laughed and patted his arm. Both of them turned Taylor's way and she offered a polite smile before turning her attention to the specials menu on a chalkboard. Takeout was definitely the way to go here. This wasn't her town or her people. She stuck out like a sore thumb.

She was just about to order a salad when Rhys returned. "Come on," he said, taking her elbow again. "Let's grab a seat."

"Um, I didn't really think we were going to eat together. I was just going to get something to take back with me."

"You work too hard," he said, holding out a chair for her and then moving around the table without pushing it in—polite without being over the top. "You could use some downtime."

She shifted the chair closer to the table. "Are you kidding? This is slow for me."

He raised his eyebrows. "Then you really do need to stop and refuel."

He shrugged out of his jacket and hooked it over the top of the chair. She did the same, unbuttoning the black-and-red wool coat and shoving her scarf in the sleeve. She wore skinny jeans tucked into her favorite boots—red designer riding boots—and a snug black cashmere sweater from an expensive department store in the city. She looked around. Most of the men wore thirty-dollar jeans and plaid flannel, and the women dressed in a similar fashion—jeans and department store tops.

Just as she thought. Sore thumb.

When she met Rhys's gaze again she found his sharper, harder, as if he could read her thoughts. She dropped her gaze and opened her menu.

"No need for that. Couple orders of pot roast are on their way."

She put down the menu and folded her hands on the top. While the rest of the decorations at the diner bordered on cheesy, she secretly loved the small silk poinsettia pots with Merry Christmas picks. "What amusement are you getting out of this?" she asked. "From what I can gather you don't approve of me but you do enjoy bossing me around."

"Why would you think that?"

"Oh, I don't know. Because so far you've found fault with everything I say or do?"

"Then why did you come with me?"

"You didn't leave me much choice." She pursed her lips.

"You always have a choice," he replied, unrolling his cutlery from his paper napkin.

"Then I guess because I was hungry," she said.

He smiled. "You mean because I was right."

Oh, he was infuriating!

"The trick is to make them want to do what I want." He repeated his earlier sentiment, only she understood he wasn't talking about horses anymore. He'd played her like a violin.

She might have had some choice words only their meals arrived, two plates filled with roast beef, potatoes, carrots, peas and delightfully puffy-looking Yorkshire puddings. Her potatoes swam in a pool of rich gravy and the smell coming from the food was heaven in itself.

She never ate like this anymore. Wondered if she could somehow extract the potatoes from the gravy or maybe just leave the potatoes altogether—that would probably be better.

"Thanks, Mom," she heard Rhys say, and her gaze darted from her plate up to his face and then to the woman standing beside the table—the same woman who had patted his arm in the kitchen. Taylor guessed her to be somewhere around fifty, with dark brown hair like Rhys's, only cut in an efficient bob and sprinkled with a few gray hairs.

"You're welcome," she said, then turned to Taylor with a smile. "You're Callum's sister. I remember you from the christening party."

Right. Taylor had flown in for that and she'd helped arrange a few details like the outdoor tent, but she'd done it all by phone from Vancouver. "Oh, my goodness, I totally didn't put two and two together. Martha Bullock... of course. And you're Rhys's mother." She offered an uncertain smile. Usually she didn't forget details like that. Then again the idea of the gruff cowboy calling anyone "Mom" seemed out of place.

"Sure am. Raised both him and his brother, Tom. Tom's been working up north for years now, but Rhys moved home a few years back."

"Your chicken tartlets at the party were to die for," Taylor complimented. "And I had the soup yesterday. You're a fabulous cook, Mrs. Bullock. Whoever your boys marry have big shoes to fill to keep up with Mom's home cooking."

Martha laughed while, from the corner of her eye, Taylor could see Rhys scowl. Good. About time he felt a bit on the back foot since he'd been throwing her off all day.

"Heh, good luck," Martha joked. "I'm guessing groomsman is as close to the altar as Rhys is gonna get. He's picky."

She could almost see the steam come out of his ears, but she took pity on him because she'd heard much the same argument from her own family. It got wearisome after a while. Particularly from her father, who'd never taken her business seriously and seemed to think her sole purpose in life was to settle down and have babies.

Not that she had anything against marriage or babies. But she'd do it on her own timetable.

"Well," she said, a bit softer, "it seems to me that getting married is kind of a big deal and a person would have to be awfully sure that they wanted to see that person every day for the rest of their lives. Not a thing to rush, really."

Martha smiled and patted Taylor's hand. "Pretty *and* wise. Don't see that very often, at least around here." She sent a pointed look at a nearby table where Taylor spied an animated blonde seated with a young man who seemed besotted with her.

"Well, your supper's getting cold." Martha straightened. "And I've got to get back. See you in a bit."

Taylor watched Rhys's mother move off, stopping at several tables to say hello. Her full laugh was infectious and Taylor found herself smiling.

When she turned back, Rhys had already started cutting into his beef. Taylor mentally shrugged and speared a bright orange carrot with her fork.

"So," she said easily. "How'd a nice woman like your mother end up with a pigheaded son like you?"

CHAPTER TWO

TENDER AS IT WAS, Rhys nearly choked on the beef in his mouth. Lord, but Callum's sister was full of sass. And used to getting her own way, too, from the looks of it. He'd noticed her way back in the fall at the christening, all put together and pretty and, well, bossy. Not that she'd been aggressive. She just had one of those natural take-charge kind of ways about her. When Taylor was on the job, things got done.

He just bet she was Student Council president in school, too. And on any other committee she could find.

He'd been the quiet guy at the back of the class, wishing he could be anywhere else. Preferably outside. On horse-back.

Burl Ives was crooning on the jukebox now and Taylor was blinking at him innocently. He wasn't sure if he wanted to be offended or laugh at her.

"She only donated half the genetic material," he replied once he'd swallowed. "Ask her. She'll tell you my father was a stubborn old mule."

Taylor popped a disc of carrot into her mouth. "Was?"

"He died when I was twenty-four. Brain aneurism. No warning at all."

"God, Rhys. I'm sorry."

He shrugged again. "It's okay. We've all moved well beyond the shock and grief part to just missing him." And he did. Even though at times Rhys had been frustrated with his father's decisions, he missed his dad's big laugh and some of the fun things they'd done as kids—like camping and fishing. Those were the only kinds of vacations their family had ever been able to afford.

They ate in silence for a while until it grew uncomfortable. Rhys looked over at her. He wasn't quite sure what had propelled him to bring her here tonight. It had been the gentlemanly thing to do but there was something else about her that intrigued him. He figured it was probably the way she challenged him, how she'd challenged them all today. He'd nearly laughed out loud during the fitting. He could read people pretty well and she had pushed all the right buttons with Callum. And then there was the way she was used to being obeyed. She gave an order and it was followed. It was fun putting her off balance by taking charge.

And then there was the indisputable fact that she was beautiful.

Except he really wasn't interested in her that way. She was so not his type. He was beer and she was champagne. He was roots and she was wings.

Still. A guy might like to fly every once in a while.

"So," he invited. "Tell me more about what you do."

"Oh. Well, I plan private parties and events. Not generally weddings. Right now, in addition to Callum and Avery's details, I'm going back and forth with my assistant about a New Year's party we're putting together. The hardest part is making sure the construction of the giant aquariums is completed and that the environment is right for the fish."

"Fish?"

She laughed, the expression lighting up her face. "Okay,

so get this. They want this under the sea theme so we're building two aquariums and we've arranged to borrow the fish for the night. It's not just the aquariums, it's the marine biologist I have coming to adjust conditions and then monitor the water quality in the tank and ensure the health of the fish. Then there are lights that are supposed to make it look like you're underwater, and sushi and cocktails served by mermaids and mermen in next to no clothing."

"Are you joking?"

She shook her head. "Would I joke about a thing like that? It's been a nightmare to organize." She cut into her slab of beef and swirled it around the pool of gravy. "This is so good. I'm going to have to do sit-ups for hours in my room to work this off."

He rolled his eyes. Right. To his mind, she could gain a few pounds and no one would even notice. If anything, she was a little on the thin side. A few pounds would take those hinted-at curves and make them...

He cleared his throat.

"What about you, Rhys? You said you work with horses?" Distracted by the chatting now, she seemed unaware that she was scooping up the mashed potatoes and gravy she'd been diligently avoiding for most of the meal.

"I work for Ty out at Diamondback."

"What sort of work?"

"Whatever has to be done, but I work with training the horses mostly. Ty employs a couple of disadvantaged people to help around the place so I get to focus on what I do best."

"What sort of disadvantaged people?" She leaned forward and appeared genuinely interested.

Rhys finished the last bite of Yorkshire pudding and nudged his plate away. "Well, Marty has Down's syndrome. Getting steady work has been an issue, but he's very good with the animals and he's a hard worker. Josh is a different story. He's had trouble finding work due to his criminal record. Ty's helping him get on his feet again. Josh helps Sam's end of things from time to time. Those cattle you mentioned herding earlier."

Taylor frowned and pushed her plate away. She'd made a solid dent in the meal and his mother hadn't been stingy with portions.

"So what are your plans, then?"

"What do you mean?"

She wiped her mouth with a paper napkin. "I mean, do you have any plans to start up your own place or business?"

"Not really. I'm happy at Diamondback. Ty's a good boss."

She leaned forward. "You're a take-charge kind of guy. I can't see you taking orders from anyone. Don't you want to be the one calling the shots?"

Calling the shots wasn't all it was cracked up to be. Rhys had seen enough of that his whole life. Along with being the boss came a truckload of responsibility, including the chance of success and the probability of failure. His own venture had cost him financially but it had been far worse on a deeper, personal level. Considering he now had his mom to worry about, he was content to leave the risk to someone else from here on in. "I have a job doing something I like and I get a steady paycheck every two weeks. What more could I want?"

She sat back, apparently disappointed with his answer. Too bad. Living up to her expectations wasn't on his agenda and he sure wasn't about to explain.

Martha returned bearing two plates of apple pie. "How was it?" she asked, looking at Taylor expectantly.

"Delicious," she had the grace to answer with a smile.

"I was trying to be good and avoid the potatoes and I just couldn't. Thank you, Martha."

"Well, you haven't had my pie yet. It's my specialty."

"Oh, I couldn't possibly."

"If it's your waistline worrying you, don't. Life's too short." She flashed a grin. "Besides, you'll wear that off running all over town. I heard you're kicking butt and taking names planning this wedding. Everyone's talking about it."

Apparently Taylor found that highly complimentary and not at all offensive. "Well, maybe just this once."

Martha put down the plates. "Rhys? The faucet in my kitchen sink at home has been dripping. I wondered if you could have a look at it? Consider dinner your payment in advance."

He nodded, knowing that last part was for Taylor's benefit more than his. He never paid for meals at the diner and instead looked after the odd jobs here and at his mother's home.

It was why he'd come back to Cadence Creek, after all. He couldn't leave his mother here to deal with everything on her own. She'd already been doing that for too many years. It had always been hand to mouth until this place. She still worked too hard but Rhys knew she loved every single minute.

"I'll be around tomorrow before work to have a look," he promised. "Then I can pick up what I need from the hardware and fix it tomorrow night."

"That sounds great. Nice to see you again, Taylor. Can't wait to see your handiwork at this wedding."

Rhys watched Taylor smile. She looked tired but the smile was genuine and a pleasant surprise. She had big-city girl written all over her but it didn't mean she was devoid of warmth. Not at all.

When Martha was gone he picked up his fork. "Try the pie. She'll be offended if you don't."

Taylor took a bite and closed her eyes. "Oh, my. That's fantastic."

"She makes her own spice blend and doesn't tell anyone what it is. People have been after her recipes for years," he said, trying hard not to focus on the shape of her lips as her tongue licked a bit of caramelly filling from the corner of her mouth. "There's a reason why the bakery focuses on cakes and breads. There's not a pie in Cadence Creek that can hold a candle to my mom's."

"You seem close," Taylor noted.

She had no idea. Rhys focused on his pie as he considered exactly how much to say. Yes, he'd come back to Cadence Creek to be nearer his mom after his dad's death. She'd needed the help sorting out their affairs and needed a shoulder. He'd been happy to do it.

But it was more than that. They were business partners. Not that many people were aware of it and that was how he wanted it to stay. Memories were long and his father hadn't exactly earned a stellar business reputation around town. Despite his best intentions, Rhys had followed in his footsteps. Being a silent partner in the restaurant suited him just fine.

"We are close," he admitted. "Other than my brother, I'm the only family she's got and the only family here in Cadence Creek. How about you? Are you close with your family?"

She nodded, allowing him to neatly change the subject. "I suppose so. We don't live so close together, like you do, but it's close enough and we get along. I know they were very worried about Callum when he came back from overseas. And they thought he was crazy for buying a dairy farm." She laughed a little. "But they can see he's happy and that's all that matters."

"And Jack?"

She laughed. "Jack is in Montana most of the time, busy overseeing his empire. We don't see each other much. Our jobs keep us very busy. Running our own businesses is pretty time-consuming."

"I can imagine." Rhys had met and liked Jack instantly, but like Taylor, he looked a bit exhausted. Running a big sporting goods chain was likely to have that effect.

Which was why Rhys was very contented to work for Diamondback and spend some of his spare hours playing handyman for the diner and his mother's house. It was straightforward. There was little chance of disappointing people.

Angry words and accusations still bounced around in his brain from time to time. Failing had been bad enough. But he'd let down the person he'd trusted most. And she'd made sure he knew it.

The fluted crust of Taylor's pie was all that remained and she'd put down her fork.

"Well, I suppose we should get going."

"I'm going to have to roll back to the B&B," she said ruefully, putting a hand on her tummy.

"Not likely," he said, standing up, but their gazes met and he was certain her cheeks were a little redder than they'd been before.

He took her coat from the back of the chair, pulled the scarf from the sleeve and held it so she could slide her arms into it. They were quiet now, he unsure of what to say and his show of manners making things slightly awkward. Like this was a date or something. He stood back and grabbed his jacket and shoved his arms in the sleeves. Not a date. It was just sharing a meal with…

With a woman.

Hmm.

"I'm putting my gloves on this time," she stated with a cheeky smile.

"Good. Wouldn't want your fingertips to fall off."

They gave a wave to Martha before stepping outside into the crisp air.

It had warmed a bit, but that only meant that the pre-cipitation that had held off now floated lazily to the earth. Big white flakes drifted on the air, hitting the ground with a soft shush of sound that was so peculiar to falling snow. It draped over hedges and windows, painting the town in fairy-white.

"This is beautiful," Taylor whispered. "Snow in Van-couver is cause for chaos. Here, it's peaceful."

"Just because the wind isn't blowing and causing white-outs," Rhys offered, but he was enchanted too. Not by the snow, but by her. The clever and efficient Taylor had tilted her head toward the sky and stuck out her tongue, catch-ing a wide flake on its tip.

"I know it's just water, but I swear snow tastes sweet for some reason," she said, closing her eyes. Another flake landed on her eyelashes and she blinked, laughing as she wiped it away. "Oops."

Rhys swallowed as a wave of desire rolled through him. Heavens above, she was pretty. Smart and funny, and while an absolute Sergeant Major on the job, a lot more relaxed when off the clock. He had the urge to reach out and take her hand as they walked through the snow. Odd that he'd have such an innocent, pure thought when the other side of his brain wondered if her mouth would taste like apples and snowflakes.

He kept his hand in his pocket and they resumed strolling.

It only took a few minutes to reach the bed and breakfast. Rhys paused outside the white picket gate. "Well, here we are."

"Yes, here we are. What about you? You walked me back but now do you have to walk home in the snow? Or are you parked nearby?" She lifted her chin and Rhys smiled at the way the snow covered her hair with white tufts. She looked like a young girl, bundled up in her scarf and coat with snow on her head and shoulders. Definitely not like a cutthroat businesswoman who never had to take no for an answer.

"I live a few blocks over, so don't worry about me."

"Do you—" she paused, then innocently widened her eyes "—live with your mother?"

He laughed. "God, no. I'm thirty years old. I have my own place. I most definitely do not live with my mother."

Her cold, pink cheeks flushed even deeper. "Oh. Well, thanks for dinner. I guess I'll see you when we pick up the tuxes, right?"

"I guess so. See you around, Taylor."

"Night."

She went in the gate and disappeared up the walk, her ruby-red boots marking the way on the patio stones.

He had no business thinking about his friend's sister that way. Even less business considering how different they were. Different philosophies, hundreds of kilometers between them... He shouldn't have taken her elbow in his hand and guided her along.

But the truth was the very thing that made her wrong for him was exactly what intrigued him. She wasn't like the other girls he knew. She was complicated and exciting, and that was something that had been missing from his life for quite a while.

As the snowfall picked up, he huddled into the collar

of his jacket and turned away. Taylor Shepard was not for him. And since he wasn't the type to mess around on a whim that meant keeping his hands off—for the next two weeks or so.

He could do that. Right?

Taylor had left the planning for the bridal shower to Clara Diamond, Ty's wife and one of Avery's bridesmaids. Tonight Taylor was attending only as a guest. In addition to the bridal party, Molly Diamond's living room was occupied by Melissa Stone, her employee Amy, and Jean, the owner of the Cadence Creek Bakery and Avery's partner in business.

In deference to Clara's pregnancy and the fact that everyone was driving, the evening's beverages included a simple punch and hot drinks—tea, coffee, or hot cocoa. Never one to turn down chocolate, Taylor helped herself to a steaming mug and took a glorious sip. Clara had added a dollop of real whipped cream to the top, making it extra indulgent. Taylor made a mental note to start running again when she returned home.

"I hope everything's okay for tonight," Clara said beside her. "It's a bit nerve-racking, you know. I can't put on an event like you, Taylor."

Taylor had been feeling rather comfortable but Clara's innocent observation made her feel the outsider again. "Don't be silly. It's lovely and simple which is just as it should be. An event should always suit the guests, and this is perfect."

"Really?"

Indeed. A fire crackled in the fireplace and the high wood beams in the log-style home made it feel more like a winter lodge than a regular home. The last bridal shower she'd attended had been in a private room at a club and they'd had their own bartender mixing custom martinis. She actually enjoyed this setting more. But it wasn't what people expected from her, was it? Did she really come across as…well…stuck up?

Taylor patted her arm. "Your Christmas decorations are lovely, so why would you need a single thing? Don't worry so much. This cocoa is delicious and I plan on eating my weight in appetizers and sweets."

She didn't, but she knew it would put Clara at ease. She liked Clara a lot. In fact she liked all of Callum's friends. They were utterly devoid of artifice.

Clara's sister-in-law Angela was taking puff pastries out of the oven and their mother-in-law Molly was putting out plates of squares and Christmas cookies. Jean had brought chocolate doughnut holes and Melissa was taking the cling wrap off a nacho dip. The one woman who didn't quite fit in was Amy, who Taylor recognized as the young woman from the diner the night she'd had dinner with Rhys. The implication had been made that Amy wasn't pretty *and* smart. But she looked friendly enough, though perhaps a little younger than the rest of the ladies.

She approached her casually and smiled. "Hi, I'm Taylor. You work for Melissa, right? I've seen you behind the counter at the shop."

Amy gave her a grateful smile. "Yes, that's right. And you're Callum's sister." She looked down at Taylor's shoes. "Those are Jimmy Choos, aren't they?"

Taylor laughed at the unconcealed longing in Amy's voice. "Ah, a kindred spirit. They are indeed."

"I'd die for a pair of those. Not that there's anywhere to buy them here. Or that I could afford them."

Her response was a bit guileless perhaps but she hadn't meant any malice, Taylor was sure of that. "I got them for a steal last time I was in Seattle," she replied. She leaned forward. "I'm dying to know. Why is it that everyone else is over there and you're over here staring at the Christmas tree? I mean, it's a nice tree, but..." She let the thought hang.

Amy blushed. "Oh. Well. I'm sure it was a polite thing to include me in the invitation. I'm not particularly close with the Diamond women. I kind of, uh..."

She took a sip of punch, which hid her face a little. "I dated Sam for a while and when he broke it off I wasn't as discreet as I might have been about it. I have a tendency to fly off the handle and think later."

Taylor laughed. "You sound like my brother Jack. Callum was always the thinker in the family. Jack's far more of a free spirit."

"It was a long time ago," Amy admitted. "It's hard to change minds in a town this size, though."

"You haven't thought of moving?"

"All the time!" Amy's blond curls bounced. "But my family is here. I didn't go to college. Oh, I must sound pathetic," she bemoaned, shaking her head.

"Not at all. You sound like someone who simply hasn't found the right thing yet. Someday you will. The perfect thing to make you want to get up in the morning. Or the perfect person." She winked at Amy.

"I'm afraid I've pretty much exhausted the local resources on that score," Amy lamented. "Which doesn't exactly make me popular among the women, either."

"You just need an image makeover," Taylor suggested. "Do you like what you're doing now?"

She shrugged. "Working for Melissa has been the best job I've ever had. But it's not exactly a challenge."

Wow. Amy did sound a lot like Jack.

"We should meet up for coffee before I go back to Vancouver," Taylor suggested. Despite the fact that Amy was included but not quite included, Taylor liked her. She just seemed young and without direction. Heck, Taylor had been there. What Amy needed was something to feel passionate about.

"I'd like that. Just stop into the shop. I'm there most days. It's busy leading up to the holidays."

The last of the guests arrived and things got underway. Taylor was glad the shower stayed on the sweeter rather than raunchier side. There was no paté in the shape of the male anatomy, no gag gifts or handcuffs or anything of the sort. They played a "Celebrity Husband" game where each guest put a name of a celebrity they had a crush on into a bowl and then they had to guess which star belonged to whom. The resulting laughter from names ranging from Kevin Costner who got Molly's vote to Channing Tatum— Amy's pick—broke the ice beautifully.

The laughter really picked up during Bridal Pictionary, which pitted Taylor against Angela as they attempted to draw "wedding night" without getting graphic. After they took a break to stuff themselves with snacks, they all returned to the living room for gifts.

Taylor sat back into the soft sofa cushions and examined the woman who was about to become her sister-in-law. Avery was so lovely—kind and gentle but with a backbone of steel. She was a fantastic mother to her niece, Nell, who was Callum's biological daughter. Taylor couldn't have handpicked a nicer woman to marry her brother. It gave her a warm feeling, but also an ache in her heart, too. That ache unsettled her a bit, until she reminded herself that she was simply very happy that Callum had found someone after all his troubles. A love like that didn't come along every day.

Her thoughts strayed to Rhys for a moment. The man was a contradiction for sure. On one hand he was full of

confidence and really quite bossy. And yet he was satisfied
with taking orders from someone else and moving back to
this small town with very few options. It didn't make sense.

It also didn't make sense that for a brief moment earlier
in the week, she'd had the craziest urge to kiss him. The
snow had been falling on his dark cap of hair and dusting
the shoulders of his jacket. And he'd been watchful of her,
too. There'd been something there, a spark, a tension of
some sort. Until he'd turned to go and she'd gone up the
walk and into the house.

She hadn't seen him since. Not at the diner, not around
town.

Avery opened a red box and a collective gasp went up
from the group. "Oh, Molly. Oh, gosh." Avery reached into
the tissue paper and withdrew a gorgeous white satin-and-
lace nightgown. "It's stunning."

"Every woman should have something beautiful for
their wedding night," Molly said. "I saw it and couldn't
resist."

Taylor watched as Avery stood and held the long gown
up to herself. The bodice was cut in a daring "V" and con-
sisted of sheer lace while the satin skirt fell straight to the
floor, a deep slit cut to the hip. It blended innocence with
sexy brilliantly.

She took another sip of cocoa and let her mind carry
her away for a few blissful seconds. What would it be like
to wear that nightgown? She would feel the lace cups on
her breasts, the slide of the satin on her thighs. She'd wear
slippers with it, the kind of ridiculous frippery that con-
sisted of heels and a puff of feathers at the toe. And Rhys's
dark eyes would light up as she came into the room, their
depths filled with fire and hunger…

"*Helloooo,* earth to Taylor!"

She blinked and focused on the circle of women who were now staring at her. "Oh. Sorry."

"I was just going to say thank you for the bath basket, but you were in another world." Avery was smiling at her.

"You're welcome! Goodness, sorry about that. Occupational hazard. Sometimes it's hard to shut the old brain off." She hoped her flippant words were believable. What would they say if they knew she'd been daydreaming about the only groomsman who wasn't married or a relative?

"Right," Amy said with a wide grin. "I know that look. You were thinking about a dude."

Damn her for being astute. Who had said she wasn't smart, anyway?

Melissa burst out laughing. "Were you? Come on, do tell. Do you have some guy hiding away in Vancouver?"

"No!" The word was out before she realized it would have been the most convenient way out of the situation.

Avery came to her rescue, though. "We're just teasing. Seriously, thank you. It's a lovely gift."

She reached for the last present on the pile and removed the card. "Oh," she said with delight. "It's from Martha. I wonder if she's going to part with her coconut cream pie recipe." Everyone laughed. Martha Bullock never shared her pie recipes with anyone. Even Rhys had mentioned that at dinner the other night.

Avery ripped the paper off the box and withdrew a plain black binder. Opening the cover, she gasped. "It *is* recipes! Look!" She read off the table of contents. "Supper Dishes, Breads and Muffins, Cookies, Cakes, Salads, Preserves." She lifted her head and laughed. "No pies."

Excited, she began flipping through the pages when Amy interrupted again. "That's it!" she called out, causing Avery's fingers to pause and the rest of the group to stare at her in surprise.

"That's where I saw you last," Amy continued, undaunted. "It was at the diner. You had dinner with Rhys!"

Six more sets of eyes swiveled Taylor's way until she felt like a bug under a microscope.

"It wasn't a date. We both ended up needing to eat at the same time. We just met outside on the sidewalk and, uh, sat together."

"It sure didn't look that way," Amy answered, a little too gleeful for Taylor's liking. "Now that is news. Rhys hasn't shown up anywhere with a date since…"

She suddenly blushed and turned her gaze to something over Jean's shoulder. "Well, it doesn't matter how long since."

It was uncomfortably quiet for a few moments until a small giggle broke the silence. Clara was trying not to laugh and failing miserably. Angela and Molly joined in, followed by Jean and Melissa. Even Avery's mouth was twitching. Taylor frowned a little, wondering what the joke could be.

Amy had the grace to look chagrined. "Okay, I know. My track record sucks."

Angela spoke up. "Honey, Rhys Bullock is one tough nut to crack. Someday the right guy's gonna come along."

Amy's eyes glistened. "Just my luck I won't recognize him when I see him."

Everyone laughed again.

Then Avery spoke up. "That's what I thought, too, Amy. Don't give up hope. You just never know." She looked at Taylor. "And I know for a fact that Rhys is smart and stubborn. Sounds like someone else I know. Keep us posted, Taylor."

"Yeah," Clara added, her hand on her rounded stomach. "The old married women need some excitement now and again."

"I swear I bumped into him outside. Literally. Ran smack into him and nearly broke my phone." She brought her hands together in demonstration of the collision. "It was dark, it was dinnertime and we had pot roast. End of story."

But as the subject changed and they cleaned up the paper and ribbons, Taylor's thoughts kept drifting back to that night and how she'd almost reached out to take his hand as he walked her home.

It was such a simple and innocent gesture to think about, especially in these days of casual hookups. Not that hooking up was her style, either. That philosophy combined with her long hours meant she hadn't had time for personal relationships for ages. Not since the early days of her business, when she'd been seeing an investment planner named John. He'd wanted more than a girlfriend who brought work home at the end of a twelve-hour day and considered takeout a sensible dinner. After a few months in, he'd walked. The thing Taylor felt most guilty about was how it had been a relief.

She balled up used napkins and put them in the trash. Time kept ticking. A few days from now was the rehearsal, and then the wedding and then Callum and Avery would be away on their honeymoon and Taylor would move out of the B&B and into their house until Boxing Day, where she planned on watching movies, reading books and basically hibernating from the outside world. It was going to be peace and quiet and then a family Christmas.

Complications in the form of Rhys Bullock would only ruin her plans.

CHAPTER THREE

IT WAS TAYLOR'S experience that if the rehearsal went badly, the wedding was sure to be smooth and problem free. A sentiment which boded well for Callum and Avery, as it turned out, because nothing seemed to be going her way.

First of all, everything was an hour late starting thanks to a winter storm, which dumped enough snow to complicate transportation. The minister had slid off the road and into a snowbank. The car wasn't damaged but by the time the tow truck had pulled him out, the wedding party was waiting and quite worried by his absence. Then Taylor opened the box that was supposed to contain the tulle bows for the ends of the church pews to find that they'd been constructed of a horrible peachy-yellow color—completely unsuited for a Christmas wedding!

The late start and the road conditions also meant canceling the rehearsal dinner that had been organized at an Italian place in the city. Taylor was just about ready to pull her hair out when she felt a wide hand rest on her shoulder.

"Breathe," Rhys commanded. "It's all fine."

She clenched her teeth but exhaled through her nose. "Normally I would just deal with stuff like this without batting an eyelid. I don't know why it's throwing me so much."

"Maybe because it's for your brother," he suggested.

He might be right. She did want everything just right for Callum's wedding. It wasn't some corporate dinner or celebrity party. It was personal. It was once in a lifetime.

God, there was a reason why she didn't do weddings.

"What can I do to help?"

She shrugged. "Do you have a roll of white tulle in your pocket? Perhaps a spare horseshoe I could rub for good luck or something?"

He grimaced. "Afraid not. And you rub a rabbit's foot, not a horseshoe. I'm guessing our plans for dinner have changed."

She looked up at him. He was "dressed up" for the rehearsal—neat jeans, even with a crease down the front, and a pressed button-down shirt tucked into the waistband. His boots made him look taller than ever, especially as she'd decided on her low-heeled boots tonight in deference to the weather. There was a strength and stability in him that made her take a deep breath and regroup. For some reason she didn't want to appear incapable in front of him. "I've had to cancel our reservations."

"I'll call my mom. It won't be as fancy as what you planned, but I'm guessing she can manage a meal for a dozen of us."

"We can't have a rehearsal dinner at a diner."

His lips puckered up like he'd tasted something sour. "Do you have any better suggestions? I guess you could pick up some day-old sandwiches at the gas station and a bag of cookies. You don't exactly have a lot of options."

"It was supposed to be romantic and relaxing and…" She floundered a little. "You know. Elegant."

He frowned at her and she regretted what she'd implied. "What would you do if you were in Vancouver right now?" he asked.

"This kind of weather wouldn't happen in Vancouver."

He made a disgusted sound. "You're supposed to be so good at your job. You're telling me nothing ever goes off the plan?"

"Well, sure it does, but I…"

"But you what?"

"I handle it."

"How is this different?"

"Because it's family."

The moment she said it her throat tightened. This wasn't just another job. This was her big brother's wedding. This was also the chance where she would prove herself to her family. She could talk until she was blue in the face, but the truth of the matter was she still sought their approval. The Shepards were driven and successful. It was just expected. She knew she'd disappointed her dad in particular. He thought what she did was unimportant, and the last thing she wanted to do was fall on her professional face in front of him.

"This isn't Vancouver, or Toronto, or New York or L.A." Rhys spoke firmly. "This isn't a big-city event with a bunch of rich snobs. It's just Cadence Creek. Maybe it's not good enough for you but it's good enough for Callum and Avery and maybe you should consider that instead of only thinking about yourself."

His words hurt. Partly because he was judging her without even knowing her and partly because he was right, at least about things being simpler here. How many times had Avery said they didn't need anything fancy? Taylor had insisted because it was no trouble. Had she messed up and forgotten the singular most important rule: *Give the client what they ask for?*

"Call your mother, then, and see if there's any way she can squeeze us in."

"Give me five minutes."

The words weren't said kindly, and Taylor felt the sting of his reproof. Still, she didn't have time to worry about Rhys Bullock—there was too much left to do. While the minister spoke to Avery and Callum, Taylor fished poinsettia plants out of a waiting box and lined them up on the altar steps in alternating red and creamy white. The congregation had already decorated the tree and the Christmas banners were hung behind the pulpit. The manger from the Sunday School play had been tucked away into the choir loft, which would be unused during the wedding, and instead she set up a table with a snowy-white cloth and a gorgeous spray of red roses, white freesias and greenery. It was there that the bride and groom would sign the register.

The altar looked fine, but the pews and windowsills were naked. In addition to the wrong color tulle, the company had forgotten to ship the candle arrangements for the windows. This would be the last time she ever used them for any of her events!

Her father, Harry, approached, a frown creasing his brow. "What are the plans for after the rehearsal?"

Taylor forced a smile. She would not get into it with her father tonight. "I'm working on that, don't worry."

"You should have insisted on having the wedding in the city, at a nice hotel. Then the weather wouldn't be an issue. Everything at your fingertips."

She'd had the thought a time or two herself; not that she'd admit it to her father. "This will be fine."

He looked around. "It would have been so much easier. Not that the town isn't nice, of course it is. But you're the planner, Taylor." His tone suggested she wasn't doing a very good job of it.

"It wasn't what Callum and Avery wanted," she reminded him. "And it's their day."

He smiled unexpectedly, a warm turning up of his lips

that Taylor recognized as his "sales pitch" smile. "Oh, come now. A smart businessman knows how to convince a client to come around."

Business*man*. Taylor wondered if counting to ten would help. She met her father's gaze. "Callum isn't a client, he's my brother. And he's giving you the daughter-in-law and grandkid you've wanted, so ease up."

Anything else they would have said was cut short as Rhys came back, tucking his cell phone in his pocket as he walked. "Good news. Business is slow because of the weather. Mom's clearing out that back corner and she's got a full tray of lasagna set aside."

It certainly wasn't the Caprese salad, veal Parmesan and tiramisu that Taylor had planned on, but it was convenient. She offered a polite smile. "Thank you, Rhys." At least one thing had been fixed.

"It's no trouble."

With a brief nod, Harry left the two of them alone.

"Everything okay?" Rhys asked.

She pressed a hand to her forehead. "Yeah, it's fine. Dad was just offering an unsolicited opinion, that's all."

He chuckled. "Parents are like that."

"You've no idea," she answered darkly. "I still wish I knew what to do about the pew markers. There's no time to run to Edmonton for materials to make them, even if it weren't storming. And the candles never arrived, either."

"It doesn't have to be perfect. No one will know."

His words echoed from before, the ones that said she was too good for this town. She dismissed them, because she still had a certain standard. "I'll know."

Clara heard the last bit and tapped Taylor on the shoulder. "Why don't you call Melissa and see if she can do something for the pews with satin ribbon?"

"At this late hour?"

Clara nodded. "Worst she can say is no. I have a feeling she'll try something, though. She's a whiz at that stuff. And I might be able to help you out with the windowsills."

Taylor's eyebrows pulled together. "What do you mean?"

Clara laughed. "Just trust me."

"I'm not in the habit of trusting details to other people, Clara. It's nothing personal—it's just how I work."

"Consider it a helping hand from a friend. You're going to be here before anyone else tomorrow anyway. If you don't like what I've done, you can take it out, no hard feelings." She smiled at Taylor. "I'd like to do this. For Avery. She's like family, you know?"

Rhys's hand touched Taylor's back. It was warm and felt good but Taylor got the feeling it was also a little bit of a warning. "I'm sure Taylor's very grateful for your help, Clara."

Dammit. Now he was putting words in her mouth. Perhaps it could be argued that this was "just family" but to Taylor's mind, if she couldn't manage to get the details of one small country wedding right, what did that say about her business?

Then again, in Vancouver she had staff. She could delegate. Which was pretty much what Clara was suggesting. She was just asking her to trust, sight unseen. And then there was the word "friend." She was a stranger here, a fish out of water for the most part and yet everyone seemed to accept her into their group without question. She wasn't used to that.

"Thank you, Clara," she said, but when Clara had gone she turned on Rhys. "Don't ever answer for me again."

"You were being rude."

Now he was judging her manners?

"Look, maybe Callum and Avery are family but I still

hold to a certain standard. This is my job. And it's all carefully planned down to the last detail."

She'd had things go wrong before and it wasn't pretty. She'd been determined never to fail like that again. It was why she dealt with trusted vendors and had a competent staff. She'd pulled off events ten times as complicated as this without a hitch.

Knowing it was like sprinkling salt in the wound.

He put a finger under her chin and lifted it. Considering how abrupt he'd been earlier, the tender touch surprised her. "You don't have to control everything. It'll be fine, I promise. It's okay to accept help once in a while."

"I'm not used to that."

"I know," he said gently. "You're stubborn, strong, bossy and completely competent. But things happen. Call Melissa, trust Clara, pretend to walk down the aisle for the rehearsal and then go stuff yourself with lasagna. I promise you'll feel better."

She didn't like being handled. Even if, at this moment, she suspected she needed it. It was so different being here. More relaxed, laid-back. She was used to grabbing her non-fat latte on her way to the office, not sipping from china cups in a B&B dining room while eating croissants. Maneuvering her SUV with the fold-down seats through city traffic rather than walking the two blocks to wherever. Definitely not used to men looking into her eyes and seeing past all her barriers.

Cadence Creek was a completely different pace with completely different expectations.

"Rhys? Taylor? We're ready for the walk-through," Avery called down the aisle, a happy smile on her face. Despite the wrinkles in the plans, Taylor's soon-to-be sister-in-law was beaming.

Well, if the bride wasn't worried, she wouldn't be, either. She looked up at Rhys. "I'll call Melissa when we're done. But if this goes wrong…"

"I expect I'll hear about it."

The other members of the wedding party joined them at the end of the aisle—first Clara and Ty, then Sam and Angela, Jack and Avery's friend Denise, who'd flown in from Ontario just this morning and thankfully ahead of the storm. Rhys held out his arm. "Shall we?" he asked, waiting for her to take his elbow.

She folded her hand around his arm, her fingers resting just below his elbow as they took slow steps up the aisle. It was just a silly rehearsal, so she shouldn't have a tangle of nerves going on just from a simple touch.

At the front of the church they parted ways and while Taylor slyly glanced in his direction several times, he never looked at her. Not once. He focused unerringly on what the minister was saying, and she found herself studying his strong jawline and the crisp hairline that looked as if his hair had been freshly cut.

The minister spoke to her and she jerked her attention back to the matter at hand, but she couldn't stop thinking about Rhys. It wasn't often that Taylor was intimidated by anyone, but she was by Rhys. She figured it had to be because he found her distinctly lacking in…well, in something.

What she couldn't understand was why on earth his opinion should even matter.

The Wagon Wheel was lit up, the windows glowing through the cold and very white night. Hard flakes of snow still swirled through the air, biting against Rhys's cheeks as he parked his truck in front of a growing drift.

They'd all bundled up and left the church a few minutes ago, the procession of vehicles crawling through town to the diner. There was no way they would have made it to the city for dinner. Even with the roads open, visibility was bad enough that there was a tow ban on. The smart thing was to stay put.

Taylor "Bossy-Pants" Shepard hadn't been too happy about that, though. He'd taken one look at her face and seen the stress that came from dealing with things gone wrong. It was a prime example of why he liked his life simple. If things went wrong out at Diamondback, he might get called to work but the worry belonged to Ty and Sam. Besides, his mother kept him plenty busy with things at the diner when she needed help. There were days he wished she didn't own the place. That she'd stayed on as a cook rather than buying it from the last owner. There was too much at stake, too much to lose.

Frigid air buffeted him as he hopped out of the truck and headed for the door, his head bowed down as far into his collar as possible. This storm had been a good one. Hopefully it would blow itself out by morning and nothing would get in the way of the wedding. For one, he only wanted to get dressed up in that tuxedo once. And for another, Callum and Avery deserved an incident-free day.

It was warm inside, and smelled deliciously like tomatoes and garlic and warm bread. Rhys stamped off his feet and unzipped his jacket, tucking his gloves into the pockets as he walked toward the back corner. His mom had been right. Other than a couple of truckers waiting out the bad roads, the place was empty.

He stopped and looked at the miracle she had produced in a scant hour.

The Christmas tree was lit, sending tiny pinpoints of colored light through the room. The heavy tables were pushed together to make one long banquet style set up for twelve, and they were covered with real linens in holiday red. The napkins were only paper but they were dark green and white, in keeping with Christmas colors. Thick candles sat in rings of greenery and berries—where had she come up with those?—and the candles lent an even more intimate air to the setting. But the final touch was the ice buckets on both ends, and the sparkling wineglasses at each place setting.

"What do you think?" His mother's voice sounded behind his shoulder.

"You're something, Ma," he said, shaking his head.

She frowned a little. "Do you think it'll be okay for Taylor? I know she must have had something fancier planned for the rehearsal dinner."

"You've worked a miracle on short notice. And if Taylor Shepard doesn't like it, she can…" He frowned. "Well, she can…"

"She can what, Rhys?"

Dammit. Her sweet voice interrupted him. He felt heat rush to his cheeks but when he turned around she was looking at Martha and smiling.

"Martha, how did you possibly do all this in such a short time?"

"It was slow in here and I had some help." She grinned. "Jean from the bakery sent over a cake—they were closing early anyway and she was happy to help with dessert. It's chocolate fudge."

"And wine?" Rhys watched as Taylor's eyes shone. Maybe he'd misjudged her. Maybe she'd just been stressed, because the snooty perfectionist he expected to see wasn't in attendance just now.

Or, perhaps she understood she was in a sticky place and was making the best of it. He suspected that faking it was in her repertoire of talents. His jaw tightened. When had he become so cynical? He supposed it was about the time Sherry had promised him to stick by his side—until things got dicey. Then she'd bailed—taking her two kids with her. Kids he'd grown very fond of.

You got to see someone's true colors when they were under pressure. It wasn't always pretty. Sherry hadn't even given him a chance to make things right.

He realized his mom was still speaking. "I'm not licensed, so I'm afraid it's not real wine. But the bed and breakfast sent over a couple of bottles of sparkling cider they had on hand and I put it on ice. I thought at least you could have a toast."

To Rhys's surprise, Taylor enveloped Martha in a quick hug. "I underestimated you," she said warmly. "This is perfect."

Martha shrugged but Rhys could tell she was pleased. "Heck," she replied with a flap of her hand. "That's what neighbors are for."

The rest of the wedding party arrived, complete with laughter and the sound of stomping boots. The next thing Rhys knew, he was seated at the table next to Avery's maid of honor, Denise, and things were well underway. Drinks were poured and he found himself chatting to Harry, who was on his other side. The senior Shepard was a very successful businessman, sharp as a tack and charismatic. Rhys could see a lot of his acumen and energy in Jack, the younger son, and the strength and reliability in Callum, the eldest. Rhys noticed that while Harry spoke proudly about Callum's military career and Jack's business, he didn't say much about Taylor's successes.

What about Taylor, then? She had the dark looks of the Shepard men rather than the more fair coloring of her mother, who sat across the table. But her lips were soft and full, like Mrs. Shepard's, and the dusting of freckles came from there, too. When he met Mrs. Shepard's gaze, he saw a wisdom there that he'd glimpsed in Taylor, too. Wisdom and acceptance. He guessed that it must have been hard to be a girl growing up in a household of such strong males. Had she felt pressure to keep up? Or were the expectations lower because she was female? He'd only known her a short time but he understood that she would hate to be treated as anything less than equal to her brothers. And then there was the tension he'd sensed between them at the rehearsal.

To his surprise, Taylor didn't sit at all but donned an apron and helped Martha serve the meal. When she put his plate before him, he looked up and met her eyes. "Thank you, Taylor."

"You're welcome."

She turned to move away but he reached out and caught her wrist. "What you said to my mother, that was very nice."

Her eyes met his. "I meant it. I apologize for my mood earlier. I was stressed."

"And here I thought it was because you didn't like to be told what to do."

Her eyes flashed at him for a second before mellowing, and then her lips twitched. "I do believe you're baiting me. Now stop so I can finish serving the meal."

He watched as she helped put the plates around, smiling and laughing. He'd thought her too proud for serving but she wasn't. She'd do what it took to pull off an event. There was lots of talking and laughing and toasting around the table, but Rhys frowned. Wasn't she going to sit and eat? While Martha tended to the few customers at the counter, it was Taylor who refilled bread baskets and beverages. Once he spied her in a corner, talking on her cell and gesturing with one hand. When Callum stood and offered a toast Rhys could see her in the kitchen, slicing cake onto plates.

Maybe it was her job, but it was her family, too. She was part of the wedding party, after all. And no one seemed to realize she was missing out.

When the meal was over the party broke up. Callum and Avery departed with a wave, in a hurry to get home to their daughter who was with a sitter. Mr. and Mrs. Shepard left for the bed and breakfast and Jack, being chivalrous, offered to take Denise with him, since they were all staying there anyway.

Angela and Clara offered to help tidy up, but Taylor shooed them away. "You've got Sam and Ty waiting and the kids at home. Go. This won't take but a minute anyway. I'll see you in the morning."

They didn't put up much of an argument, Rhys noticed. Clara put a hand on her swollen tummy and looked relieved.

As they were leaving, another group of truckers came in, looking for hot coffee and a meal before calling it a night. Martha bustled around, attending to them—Rhys knew that on a night like tonight, the tips would be generous.

Meanwhile Taylor grabbed a plastic dishpan and was loading up dirty plates.

She'd missed the entire celebration and was left to clean up the mess. He was pretty sure this wasn't in the job description, and he was annoyed on her behalf. Her family had been utterly thoughtless tonight.

He went around to the opposite side of the table and began stacking plates.

"What are you doing?"

Clank, clank. The flatware clattered on the porcelain as he picked up the dishes. "Helping."

"I got this, Rhys."

He took the stack over to her and put it in the dishpan. "Well, you shouldn't."

"Sorry?"

She looked tired. Tiny bits of hair had come out of her braid and framed her face, and her eyes looked slightly red and weary. "Have you even eaten, Taylor?"

"I'll get something later."

Lord, she was stubborn. "There's no one here now to know that this is your job, because I know that's what you're going to say. And you know what? This isn't your job. For Pete's sake."

"Are you angry at me? Because I'm not leaving all this for Martha. It *is* my job, Rhys. When I plan an event, I sometimes have to chip in and help where it's needed. Even if it's taking out trash or clearing dishes or providing someone with a spare pair of panty hose."

"Not this time. And no, I'm not angry at you."

She lifted her chin. "Then why are you yelling at me? People are staring."

He looked over. Martha was pretending not to watch but he could tell she was paying attention. The truckers weren't so discreet. They were openly staring.

He sighed. "I'm angry at your family. They never even noticed that you didn't sit down. Callum gave the toast without you. And other than Clara and Angela, everyone left without so much as an offer to help clean up. If everyone had pitched in…"

"They had more on their minds." Her posture had relaxed slightly. "It's okay, Rhys. Really."

"Will you go eat, please? Let me look after this."

She sighed. "Tell you what. I'll help clear the tables, and then I'll eat while you put the tables and chairs back to where they normally belong. Deal?"

He could live with that, especially since he figured Taylor wasn't one to generally compromise. "Deal."

With carols playing softly in the background, it only took a few minutes to clear the dirty dishes away. Rhys took them to the kitchen while Taylor stripped away the soiled tablecloths and put the centerpieces in a cardboard box. Together they loaded the kitchen dishwasher and then Rhys put a square of leftover lasagna on a plate, heated it in the microwave and poured Taylor a glass of ice water. When it was hot, he added a bit of salad to the side and grabbed a napkin and utensils.

"That smells delicious."

"Sit. Eat. That's an order."

He knew she was tired when she merely smiled and faked a salute as she sat at an empty table. "Yes, boss."

She'd made a good dent in the lasagna by the time he'd pushed the tables back into place and put the chairs around them. Without a word he went to the kitchen and cut a slice of that chocolate fudge cake she'd missed out on. When he took it to her, she held up her hand. "I couldn't possibly."

"Yes, you can. It's delicious."

"I have a dress to fit into tomorrow."

"Which will look beautiful." He put a bit of cake—complete with fudgy frosting—on the fork and held it out. "Trust me."

"Trust you." She raised one cynical eyebrow so brilliantly he nearly laughed. "As if."

He wiggled the fork. She leaned forward and closed her lips around it, sucking the frosting off the tines.

His body tensed simply from the intimate act of feeding her, feeling the pressure of her lips conducted through metal, the way she closed her eyes at the first rich taste. He enjoyed bantering with her. Matching wits. That didn't happen often around here. But it was more than that. There

was an elemental attraction at work. Something indefin-
able that was more than a physical response to her unusual
beauty. She was the most capable woman he'd ever met.
So why did she seem particularly vulnerable? Especially
around her family?

"That's good," she murmured, licking a bit of chocolate from her upper lip.

"I know." His voice was hoarse and he cleared his
throat. "Have another bite."

"I shouldn't."

In response he put more on the fork and held it out. She
took it, and then he took a bite for himself, feeling adoles-
cently pleased that his lips followed where hers had been.
The room seemed more silent now, and he suddenly realized that the last few customers had gone, the music had
stopped and Martha was turning out lights.

"Oh," Taylor said, alarmed. "We should go."

Martha peered through the kitchen door. "Was everything all right, Taylor?"

"It was lovely, Mrs. Bullock. Thank you so much."

"Don't thank me. You were the workhorse tonight."
When Taylor moved to stand up, Martha flapped a hand.
"Take your time. Rhys will lock up, won't you Rhys?"

"Sure thing, Ma." He never took his eyes off Taylor as
he answered. They were going to be alone—truly alone—
for the first time. Eating cake by the light of the Christmas
tree in the corner. The back door through the kitchen shut,
echoing in the silence.

"I didn't mean to…"

He shook his head. "I have keys to the place. It's okay.
I've locked up plenty of times."

"No, what I mean is…"

She stopped talking, looked into his eyes and bit down
on her lip.

She was feeling it, too. There was something. Something that had been lit the moment that she'd threatened to make him wear a cravat. She meant they shouldn't be alone.

She was probably right.

Instead he gazed into her eyes, unwilling to end the evening just yet. "Do you want some milk to go with your cake?" he asked.

CHAPTER FOUR

SHE SHOULD NEVER have had the cake. Or the milk. Or sat around actually enjoying Rhys's company as the night drew on and on and it was close to midnight and she was still so wired the thought of sleep was ludicrous.

Rhys was bossy and annoying and, at times, growly. He was also the only person to have noticed how she was excluded tonight. When she was working a job she tried to be invisible, behind the scenes. Maybe she'd done her job a little too well, then. Because she'd sure been invisible to her family this evening.

It had stung. In her head she knew she was just doing her job but in her heart it had hurt a little bit, that no one had at least asked her to pause and join the celebration. Not even for the toast.

Except Rhys had noticed.

She was getting used to the sight of his face, rugged and far less refined than most of the men she was accustomed to. Rhys wasn't pretty. But as she looked into his eyes across the table, with the lights of the tree reflected in the irises, she realized a man didn't have to be pretty to be sexy as hell.

"It's getting late. I should get back. Tomorrow's a long day." She balled up her paper napkin and put it on her dirty plate.

"You're probably right," he agreed. "I'll just put these things in the sink."

She followed him to the kitchen. "Rhys. Thank you. I know I blew it off before but it did kind of hurt. That they didn't notice, I mean."

He rinsed the plate and left it in the sink since the dishwasher was already running. "No problem."

She gave a short laugh. "Well, at least being away from the table meant I avoided the 'why aren't you married with a few kids yet' speech."

Rhys gave the kitchen a final check. "Why aren't you, by the way? Or aren't you interested in those things?"

She shrugged. "I like kids. My dad tends to think in lines of traditional roles, like who the breadwinner is and who does the nurturing."

"And you don't?"

She lifted her shoulders. "I don't. I think as long as a couple has a division of labor that works for them, then who am I to criticize? I suppose I'll settle down someday, when I have the time. After I've proved myself."

"And how will you know when you get there?"

She looked up, startled. "What do you mean?"

"I mean, how do you measure that? What do you need to check off on a list to consider yourself a success?"

She floundered. There was no list. "I guess I'll just know."

"Or maybe you'll never know. Let me hit the lights."

She thought about his words as she put on her coat. What was her "yardstick" for success? A dollar amount? Number of employees? Acceptance from her family?

She was so afraid of disappointing any of them, she realized. Callum was a decorated soldier. Jack had been an elite athlete before he'd become a businessman. She loved her brothers but it was hard to compete with their overachievements.

It was a bit of a shock to realize that she'd picked a business where she was behind the scenes, out of the limelight. Where she was protected just a little bit from visibility if she failed.

When had she become so afraid?

Rhys finished up and when they stepped outside she realized just how much snow had fallen—and it was still coming down. Her car was covered and the snowplow had been by, leaving a deep bank right behind her back bumper. She sighed. She didn't even have a shovel, just a brush in the backseat for cleaning off the windshield.

"Come on, I'll take you in the truck," Rhys said, but Taylor shook her head.

"I have to dig it out sometime and I'm due at the golf club by 9:00 a.m. in order to get everything set up for the reception."

"You try driving that little thing out there before the plows make another pass and you're sure to slide off into the ditch." He shook his head. "There aren't even snow tires on it, just all-seasons. I'll take you out there in the morning."

She didn't want to rely on Rhys too much, especially since he seemed very adept at prying into her business. "Jack's rental's a 4x4. I'm sure he'll run me out if the roads are bad."

"Suit yourself." He didn't sound too put out by her refusal, which was a relief. "But for now, you'd best let me take you home."

Home being the B&B. She didn't have a choice. There was no way her car was going to be unstuck tonight and she really didn't feel like walking through the snowdrifts at this hour.

Rhys unlocked the door to his truck and waited while she got in, then jogged around the front and hopped in the driver's side. He started the engine and let everything warm up for a few minutes while Taylor stared at the clouds her breath was making in the air.

The heater kicked in and the air around her feet began to warm. "Gosh, it's cold. I'm so used to the coast. This is full-on winter."

"Complete with whiteouts and a snow removal system that operates at the speed of a slug." Rhys grinned. "Still, with this good dump of snow there'll be lots of sledding happening over the holidays."

"Sledding?"

"Snowmobiles," he confirmed. "Lots of wide-open space here, but a lot of the guys like to go into the mountains and into the backcountry."

"That sounds like something Jack would love."

Rhys grinned. "He might have said something about coming back for a trip later this winter. If he can drag Callum away from his new bride. I get the feeling that Jack's a little more adventurous than Callum."

"Just in a different way," she replied, rubbing her gloved hands together. "Callum got all the adventure he wanted in the army, I think, and he was ready to settle down. Jack's more of a daredevil. Anyway, hopefully this will let up by the morning so nothing interferes with the wedding."

He put the truck in gear. "Right. Well, let's get you home so you can get your beauty sleep."

It took no time at all, even at crawling speed, to reach the B&B. The front porch light was on and white Christmas lights twinkled through the snow that had settled on the porch and railings. Rhys put the truck in Park and left the engine running.

Taylor faced him; saw his face illuminated by the dashboard lights. The snow on his hair had melted, making it darker than usual, almost black. Who was Rhys Bullock anyway? Horse trainer, sure. And clearly devoted to his mother, which was another plus. But what made him tick? What were his thoughts, his views? What went on in that complicated male mind of his? On one hand he claimed he didn't want to be tied down, but there was no doubt in her mind that he'd put down roots in Cadence Creek. What was that about?

Why on earth did she care?

"I, uh, thanks for the drive."

"You're welcome."

"And for making me eat. And..." She wet her lips. "Well, for noticing what no one else did."

There was an awkward pause as if he were deliberating over his next words. "You don't need to prove anything to your family, you know," he finally said quietly. "As long as you're squared away with yourself, that's all that matters."

Her lips dropped open. How could he possibly know that she'd always felt like she came up short? Her dad was always talking about how the boys made him proud. She always felt a few steps behind. There was something in Rhys's voice, too. Something that said that he was familiar with those words. Like maybe he'd said them to himself a time or two. Why?

"Rhys."

She'd unbuckled her seat belt and for several heartbeats the air in the cab held, as if wondering if she were going to stay in or get out. Their gazes met and things got ten times more complicated as neither of them seemed capable of looking away. Somehow they drifted closer. Closer...

She wanted to kiss him. The notion was strange and wonderful and slightly terrifying. Nothing could ever come of this, but he was feeling it, too. He must be, because she saw him swallow as he blindly reached around and undid his seat belt, his dark gaze never leaving hers. Nothing was holding him back now and still the fear and excitement waved over her, amplified in the small space of the truck cab. She didn't do this. She didn't get personal. And still she had the urge to touch, the desire to explore.

"You're going to have to meet me halfway," he murmured, his voice deep and inviting. There was no doubt now, was there? With those words he'd told her that they were on exactly the same page. The air between them sizzled.

"This is probably a mistake," she answered, dropping her gaze, breaking the connection. "I should go inside."

She didn't want to, though. And her pulse leaped wildly as he slid across the seat and reached out with his left hand, curling it around her hip and pulling her across the upholstery. "Hush," he said, and then cupped her cheek in that same hand. "We're both sitting here wondering, so why don't we get this out of the way?"

When his lips came down on hers, it stole her breath. Nothing could have prepared her for the warm insistence of his mouth or the reaction rocketing through her body. One taste and the whole kiss exploded into something wild and demanding. She reached out and gripped the front of his jacket and his arms came around her, pulling her so close she was nearly on his lap. A squeak escaped her lips as he looped one arm beneath her bottom and tugged so she was sprawled across his legs, cushioned by a strong arm as the kiss went on and on, her body ached with trembling need and her head was clouded with sheer desire.

Except somewhere in the fog was the understanding that this couldn't go any farther. She pulled away first, shaking with the intensity of their connection. "Wow," she whispered, their limbs still tangled. Despite the truck being left running, the windows had already fogged up as the sound of their breathing filled the cab.

He let out a soft curse. "I didn't expect that," he said, running his hand over his hair. "God, Taylor."

She had to get some of her bravado back or he'd see exactly how rattled she was. "Too much?" she asked innocently.

"Too much?" He gaped at her for a second, but she wasn't fooled. There was a fire in the dark depths of his eyes that was tremendously exciting.

His voice held a rasp that shivered over her nerve endings. "When I was eighteen I would have been digging for the condom in my wallet by now and heading for the privacy of the gravel pit."

She giggled. He had a condom in his wallet? Or did he mean hypothetically? What was most surprising was how badly she wanted to. Wanted him. That if he'd seriously asked she would have actually considered it even though she totally wasn't into casual anything.

It was too much. Too fast. "That sounds romantic," she replied, the words injected with a healthy dose of sarcasm. She pushed off his lap and back onto the seat of the truck.

"I'm not eighteen anymore," he admitted, letting out a breath. "I'd like to think I've learned some finesse since then. And a quickie in the cab of my truck..." He hesitated, let the thought linger.

Would never be enough. He didn't need to say it for her to hear the words. "I'd better go," she said, sliding all the way over to the door and grabbing her purse. Get out before she changed her mind and crawled into his arms again. "This wasn't such a good idea."

"Because I'm a small-town hick, right?"

She frowned, brought up short. Did he really think she was such a snob? "I didn't say that. It just doesn't make sense to start something when I'm only here until Boxing Day. Then I go back to my world and you stay here in yours. Anything else is just fooling ourselves, Rhys, and you know it."

There was a long, awkward silence. "I'll pick you up tomorrow morning and take you to the club," he offered, but his voice was tight, like she'd somehow offended him.

"Jack will take me."

Rhys let out a frustrated sigh. "Will you call if you need anything?"

She squared her shoulders. "I won't. Thanks for the lift. See you at the church."

She opened the door and hopped down, her boots sinking into eight inches of fresh snow. She wouldn't look back at him. He'd know. Know that if he said the right thing or made the slightest move she'd be in the middle of that bench seat, holding on to his arm as he drove out to the pit or wherever people went parking these days, snowstorm be damned. And she never did things like that. In fact, she hadn't been involved with anyone that way since John. Since he'd said all those hurtful things before slamming the door. She'd put all her energy into the business instead.

Without looking back, she started up the walk to the porch. Rhys gunned the engine the slightest bit—did "Mr. Uptight Pants" have a bit of a rebellious side after all?—and pulled away, driving off into the night.

She tiptoed up the steps and carefully opened the door—a single light glowed from the front window but Taylor expected everyone would be in bed. She'd have to apologize in the morning for coming in so late.

"Aren't you a little old to be parking?" came a voice on her right.

She jumped, pressed a hand to her heart. "Jack. What are you doing up?"

"Big brother was waiting for you. What took you so long?"

She recalled Rhys's criticism of her family and felt her temper flicker. "Someone had to stay and clean up."

"Isn't that the owner's job? What's her name? Martha?"

"Rhys's mother, yes. And considering she was a staff of one tonight and still managed to put on a great dinner for us at a moment's notice, I certainly wasn't going to walk out of there and leave her with a mess. Not that anyone else seemed to mind."

He came forward and frowned down at her. "Touchy," he remarked. "This have anything to do with why you were in Rhys's truck for so long, and with the windows steamed up?"

She didn't want to blush, but the heat crept up her neck and into her cheeks anyway. "That is none of your business."

"Be careful is all I'm saying. He's not your type."

"How would you know what my type is?"

He straightened and it seemed to her that he puffed out his chest. "Oh, I know. You go for the pretty boys who work downtown in two-thousand-dollar suits."

"Men like you, you mean?"

His eyes glittered. "Hardly. You pick guys who aren't a challenge and who don't challenge you. Guys like Rhys Bullock won't let you away with your usual tricks, sis."

She had to keep a lid on her temper before she said something she'd regret. Jack had such a tendency to be cocky and normally she just brushed it off. Tonight it irritated. Could she not do anything right? "Then how convenient for you that he just gave me a lift home after helping me clear away the dishes. Oh, and he reminded me I hadn't had time to eat at the dinner, either, and fixed me a plate. And when we finally went to leave, my rental was completely blocked in by a snowbank so he offered me a drive home. My type or not, Rhys Bullock was very supportive this evening. So you can put that in your pipe and smoke it, Jackson Frederick Shepard."

Unperturbed, Jack merely folded his arms and raised an eyebrow at her.

"I'm going to bed," she announced. "I recommend you do the same. You're taking me to the golf club at eight-thirty so I can be sure it's ready for the reception."

Without waiting for an answer, she swept up the stairs, her pride wrapped around her. It was only when she was settled in her room, dressed in flannel pajamas and curled under the covers that she let down her guard and closed her eyes.

Behind her lids she saw Rhys. And she saw what might have happened—if only they were different people, in a different place and time.

The church was beautiful.

Taylor let out a relieved sigh as she peeked through the nearly closed door leading through the sanctuary. It had taken longer than she'd anticipated, making sure the reception venue was all on schedule and then it had been time to head to Molly Diamond's, where all the bridesmaids were meeting to get ready and have pictures taken. Taylor gave the thumbs-up to the photographer, Jim, who had flown in from Victoria to do the wedding as a personal favor. He was set up at the front of the church, ready for Avery's walk down the aisle.

Taylor's worries about the decorations had been pointless. She wasn't sure how Melissa Stone had managed it, but the end of each pew held a stunning but simple decoration consisting of a red satin bow and a small cedar bough. Not only did it look festive, but the smell was incredible.

And Clara had come through with the sills, too. On each one was a small rectangular plate with three white pillar candles of varying heights. It was incredibly romantic and the warm light radiated through the church. She couldn't have come up with anything more suitable on her own.

With a lump in her throat, she turned to Clara and smiled. "How on earth did you manage that?" she asked. "It's perfect!"

Clara laughed lightly. "I called the owner of the dollar store last night and asked if we could go in early this morning."

The dollar store. Heaven forbid any of her clients ever found out! She gave an unladylike snort and patted Clara's arm. "I swear I need to stop underestimating the women of this town. First Martha with the dinner, then you with the candles and Melissa with the pew markers. I'm starting to feel rather irrelevant."

Avery heard and her face fell with concern. "Oh, don't say that, Taylor! We put this together in such a short time that if it weren't for you we'd be standing in front of the Justice of the Peace and having a potluck. I never dreamed I'd have a wedding day like this. It would never have happened without you."

Taylor's eyes stung. This was so different from anything she'd ever experienced. She hadn't even had to ask for help. Without even knowing her, people had stepped up because it was the right and neighborly thing to do. Maybe Cadence Creek wasn't the hub of excitement Taylor was used to, but never had she ever been made to feel like she belonged so easily. She was starting to understand why Callum was so happy here.

"It was my pleasure, I promise. Now let me check to see what's going on."

Because Avery had no family, they'd decided to forgo

the official ushering in of the parents. Instead Taylor's mom and dad sat at the front, with an adorable Nell, dressed in white ruffles, on their laps. Taylor turned her attention to the side door as it opened and the minister and men came through. At last night's rehearsal it had become glaringly apparent that everyone had an escort up the aisle but the bride. They'd made a quick change of plans, and the women would be walking up the aisle alone with the groomsmen waiting at the front.

Taylor's heart beat a little faster as Rhys appeared, looking so very handsome and exciting in the black tux and tie. The men lined up along their side of the altar, with Rhys positioned right after Jack. The pianist began to play Gounod's "Ave Maria," the signal for the women to begin their walk.

"This is it, girls." Taylor quickly got them in order and then took her place behind Angela. She gave the man at the door a quick nod and it opened, and the procession began.

Clara went first, radiant in dark green, glowing with pregnancy and holding her bouquet in front of her rounded tummy. Then Angela, smiling at her husband at the other end, and then, in the middle of the procession, Taylor.

She stepped on to the white runner, her emerald satin heels sinking slightly into the carpet. She kept slow time with the music, a smile on her face as she winked at her brother who was waiting rather impatiently for his bride. Jack was beside him, grinning like a fool and then…

And then there was Rhys, watching her with an intensity that made her weak at the knees. The smile on her lips flickered until she purposefully pasted it there, but she couldn't deny the jolt that had rushed through her that second their eyes met. Her chest cramped as her breath caught, and then his lips curved the tiniest bit and his gaze warmed with approval. And she was back in the truck last night, feeling his hands on her body and his lips on her lips and she got hot all over.

Then she was in her place, Denise followed and the music changed.

Taylor forgot all about Rhys the moment Avery stepped to the door and on the carpet. Her lace dress was classic and romantic, her solid red rose bouquet perfect. Taylor's throat tightened as she took one quick glance at her brother and found his eyes shining with tears. She couldn't cry. She wouldn't. She never did at these things. But today was different. She knew how Callum had had his heart broken before and how incredible it was that he was even standing here today. Nell stood on her grandfather's lap and everyone chuckled when she bounced and said "Mumm mumm mumm."

Avery reached Callum, and he held out his hand. She took it and they faced the minister together.

The prayers were short and heartfelt, the "I Do's" immediate and clear so that they echoed to the farthest pew. It was when Avery handed her bouquet to Denise and took Callum's fingers in hers that Taylor wished she'd tucked a tissue into the handle of her bouquet.

The vows were simple and traditional, the words solid and true as they filled the candlelit church. "I Callum, take you Avery, to be my wife. To have and to hold from this day forward."

A lump formed in Taylor's throat as she tried to swallow.

"For better or worse, richer or poorer, in sickness and in health."

Taylor took a fortifying breath and told herself to hold it together. But it was so hard, because she could see the look on Callum's face as he gazed into the eyes of his bride. He was so in love. So sure. The promises were the most important he'd make in his life, but they came easily because he loved Avery that much. Taylor had never experienced anything like that. Sometimes she doubted she ever would…if she was actually that…lovable.

Avery's soft, gentle voice echoed them back. "I Avery, take you Callum, to be my husband. To have and to hold, from this day forward."

A single tear splashed over Taylor's lower lashes. She was mortified.

"To love, honor and cherish for as long as I live."

The pair of them blurred as her eyes filled with moisture and she struggled not to blink. The pronunciation was made, there was clapping during the kiss, and then Avery, Callum, Denise and Jack moved to the table to sign the register and wedding certificate. Just when she was sure the tears were going to spill over, a dark figure appeared in front of her and held out a handkerchief.

She didn't need to see the fine details to know it was Rhys. Her heart gave a confused flutter just before she reached out and took the fabric from his hand. The shape of his lips curved slightly before he silently stepped back, and she gave a self-conscious laugh as she turned her head a little and dabbed at her eyes.

She could see again but she didn't dare look at him. A handkerchief—a white one, she could see now, and it smelled like starch and his aftershave. What sort of man these days carried a white handkerchief, for Pete's sake? And why on earth was she charmed by it?

The documents were signed, the minister introduced them as Mr. and Mrs. Callum Shepard and clapping erupted as the bride and groom immediately went to gather their daughter and then swept jubilantly down the aisle.

Taylor swallowed as Rhys offered his elbow. "Shall we?" he asked quietly, smiling down at her.

She tucked her hand in the crook of his elbow. It was strong and warm and she felt stupidly pretty and feminine next to him. "Certainly," she replied as they made their way out of the sanctuary to the much cooler vestibule. They'd form a receiving line there briefly, and then the guests would go on to the golf club for a cocktail hour while the wedding party had pictures taken.

Taylor gave a final sniff and prepared to get herself together. She had the next hour to get through and didn't want smudged makeup or red eyes to mar the photos. The sentimental moments had passed.

What she hadn't prepared herself for was the number of times she'd be forced close to Rhys during the photos; how she'd feel his hand rest lightly at her waist or his jaw close to her hair. By the time the wedding party was dismissed, her senses were so heightened her skin was tingling.

"You want a drive to the club?" Rhys asked, as the groomsmen and bridesmaids gathered by the coatrack.

"Avery said we could all go in the limo that brought us from Diamondback."

"But aren't they doing just some bride and groom photos in the snow first? I guess I figured you'd want to get there and make sure things were running smoothly."

She smiled up at him, making sure to put several inches between them. "You know me too well."

He shrugged. "That part's easy to read. The tears on the other hand? Total surprise." He reached for her coat and held it out so she could slip her arms into the sleeves.

"And yet you were at the ready with a hanky. Impressive." She needed to inject some humor so he wouldn't know how genuinely touched she'd been at the gesture.

He chuckled. "That was Molly's doing. She said that at weddings you never know when a woman might need a hanky. She gave one to all of us."

He brushed his hands over the shoulders of her coat before stepping back. "Didn't think it'd be you, though. You're too practical for that. I guess I figured you'd be thinking two or three steps ahead."

Normally she would have been, and it stung a bit knowing that Rhys only saw what everyone else seemed to see—a woman lacking in sentimentality. But she'd been caught up in the moment just like everyone else. And for the briefest of seconds, she'd felt a strange yearning. Like she was possibly missing out on something important.

"I slipped up," she replied, reaching in the coat pocket for a pair of gloves. "It's just temporary."

She finally looked up into his face. His dark eyes were glowing down at her and whatever other smart reply she'd been about to make fluttered away like ribbons on a breeze. Her gaze inadvertently slid to his lips as she remembered the sound of his aroused breathing in the confined space of his truck. A truck that he was suggesting she get in— again.

This time there would be no funny business. She really should get to the venue and make sure everything was going according to plan. She relaxed her face into a pleasant smile. "I'll accept the drive with thanks. Let me just tell Jack that I'm going on ahead."

"Taylor?" He stopped her from walking away by grabbing her arm, his fingers circling her wrist. "You should slip up more often. It looks good on you."

Maybe he did see more. She wasn't sure if that was a good thing or not. "I'll tell Jack," she repeated.

"I'll warm up the engine," he answered.

She turned around to find her brother and when she turned back again, a cold gust of wind from the just-opened door hit her like an icy wall.

She had to keep her head about her today. Weddings

made people do strange things. It was just as well, then, that she planned on remaining behind the scenes as much as possible.

CHAPTER FIVE

THE RECEPTION WAS going off without a hitch. When Taylor arrived at the club, the guests were already circulating and enjoying the cocktail hour. Platters of crackers, cheese and cold cuts, shrimp rings, crudités and fruit were set out on tables close to the bar, where people were lined up to be served either punch or hot cider.

The place looked lovely. The centerpieces had been lit—boy, Melissa had really outdone herself with those. White candles enclosed in glass sat on real rounds of wood, surrounded by aromatic greenery and winterberries. Each chair was covered in white fabric, a wide red ribbon around the back with more cedar and a single pinecone adding a festive, homey touch. The pew markers had mirrored the design perfectly. She couldn't have planned it any better. Hadn't, actually. Funny how some things worked out.

Rhys showed up at her elbow and handed her a cup. "Have something hot to drink."

"I should check the kitchen."

"You should relax. Maybe enjoy yourself."

"I'll enjoy myself later." But she took the mug anyway. The sweet, spicy scent of the cider was too tempting to resist.

"You look beautiful by the way," he said quietly.

Her pulse fluttered again. "Thank you," she answered

politely, but inside she glowed. She was used to dressing up, but her style usually ran to the classic and conservative. Tailored fits and solid colors that spoke far more to class, confidence and efficiency than femininity and whimsy. But the dress today made her feel very girly indeed. The bodice was strapless and the lace overskirt to the emerald tea-length gown was far more dainty than she normally wore. Not to mention the gorgeous satin shoes on her feet, or the way her hair was gathered in a low chignon with a few pieces left artfully around her face.

"Do you want something to eat? I can bring you something if you like."

What was she doing? Last night she'd lost her senses, but it was the clear light of day now. Sure, weddings brought out the romantic in anyone but she was smarter than that. This wasn't anything. One kiss in a truck at midnight didn't make them a couple today. Or any day for that matter.

"I can get it myself, you know. You don't have to act like we're a couple just because we're paired up in the wedding party," she answered, making a pretense of scanning the room even though everything was moving along seamlessly.

Her breath squeezed in her lungs as she waited for his reaction. When she didn't get one, she turned to say something only to discover that he'd walked away. He'd gone to the buffet table, and she wondered if he'd stay true to form and simply ignore her wishes. But when he'd put a few selections on his plate, he never even glanced her way. He walked over to the other side of the room, greeting a few guests with a smile.

It made no sense that she felt empty and bereft when he'd done exactly as she'd intended.

Fine. She'd go to the kitchens and check on the dinner

prep, and then make sure the sound system was a go for the emcee. That's where she should be anyway. Not trying to impress a stubborn groomsman.

The words had sat on Rhys's tongue but he'd kept them to himself. At a wedding reception was no place to tell her exactly what he thought of her rude response. But he was plenty put out. He'd only been trying to be a gentleman. Sure, he enjoyed pushing her buttons. But after last night…

Never mind that. Even if that kiss had never happened, he would have been courteous to any woman he'd been paired with for the day. That was just plain manners where he came from. But she was too damned independent. Wanted to do everything by herself. Was it to prove she could? She didn't have to prove anything to him. Anyone with eyes in their head could see she was good at her job. She'd pulled this whole event together in a few weeks. That took organizational skills and long hours and, he suspected, a good amount of money. He felt like saying, "I get it. You're successful and you earned it all by yourself."

The contrast between them was laughable. So why did he bother? He got the feeling she'd never understand his point of view anyway.

He mingled a bit, visiting with neighbors and acquaintances. The Diamonds arrived, and then fifteen minutes after that Avery and Callum followed, along with Denise and Jack and of course, the adorable Nell. His gaze lit on the little girl for a moment, all in ruffles with a tiny green bow in her dark curls. Humph. Taylor probably didn't even want kids. It would take too much time away from her business and important tasks. How much more reminding did he need that she was not for him? Her work was her top priority.

Rhys's heart constricted as he thought of the two little

boys he'd grown so attached to. For a while he'd been so focused on saving the business that he'd neglected the people closest to him. Funny how your perspective changed when you lost what you didn't appreciate in the first place.

So why did he kiss her last night? Why had he made an effort today? And why in hell couldn't he stop thinking about her eyes swimming with tears as he handed her a stupid square of cotton during the ceremony?

Sam took the mic and introduced the happy couple and asked everyone to take their seats. "You, too, Taylor," he added, glimpsing her talking to one of the wait staff by the door. She smiled and gave a little shrug, making people chuckle as she came his way.

Rhys waited. And when she got to his side, he held out his arm.

He could tell her teeth were clenched as she smiled and put her hand on his arm. "You did that on purpose," she accused, smiling brightly.

He smiled back. "Yes, I did. Just to annoy you."

Her eyes sparked. "Why would you do that?"

"Because pushing your buttons amuses me," he replied. "I know I shouldn't." He pulled out her chair with a flourish and noticed her cheeks were flushed. "It's pretty clear where we stand. But I can't resist."

She took up her napkin and gave it a sharp flap before settling it on her lap. "Hmm. I took you for a rule follower. Straight and narrow. Didn't take you as a bit of a scamp."

Once upon a time he'd been far more carefree and less careful. A risk taker. Circumstances had made him grow up in a hurry. "Funny," he answered, taking his seat and retrieving his own napkin. "I never pictured you as the sappy type either, but…"

"Maybe we bring out the worst in each other," she said in an undertone, reaching for her water glass.

"See? We're getting to know each other better. Now I know that you see both fun and sentimentality as flaws."

"You're deliberately twisting my words."

"Be quiet. The minister is going to say the blessing."

He was gratified when she clamped her lips shut—score one for him. After the blessing, Sam took to the mic again, explaining the order of the evening while the salads were served. Even the salads matched the Christmas decor—greens with candied pecans, red cranberries and creamy feta. Her attention to the smallest detail was starting to get annoying.

Staff were on hand at each table to pour the wine, and he noticed that when Taylor's glass had been filled with red, she reached for it immediately and took a long sip.

Maybe he shouldn't bug her so much. She had a lot on her mind today. He didn't need to add to the stress.

Then again, there was something to be said for distraction. And he did enjoy pushing her buttons. It was a nice break from his self-imposed "dry spell."

"Good wine?" he asked, reaching for his glass.

"One of my favorites, from Mission Hill. Do you like it?"

He did, though he wasn't much of a wine drinker. "It's okay."

"What's wrong with it?"

"Nothing. I said it was okay."

A look of understanding lit in her eyes. "You don't drink much wine, do you?"

He shrugged. "Not as a rule." When would he drink wine? It wasn't like he went on dinner dates or was the kind to chill out at the end of the day with a nice chardonnay. At her distressed look, he took pity on her. "Look, I'm a guy. Most of us around here are beer men, that's all. Which would be totally out of place at this dinner."

"Oh, is it too fancy? I tried to keep it fairly traditional. Nothing that people can't pronounce, that sort of thing, you know?"

Gone was the sharp tongue and sassy banter. She was actually concerned. A few days ago he might have taken her comment differently, like maybe she meant the people of Cadence Creek weren't as sophisticated as she was. But that wasn't it. Her brow was wrinkled in the middle. He knew without asking that she'd tried very hard to come up with a menu that people would like.

"What's the main course?" he asked.

"Beef Wellington, Duchess potatoes, green beans and roasted red pepper."

"Sounds delicious."

"Well, Avery approved it, but then she approved just about everything I suggested." Her eyes widened. "Oh, Rhys, did I railroad her into stuff? Did she feel she couldn't say no?"

"Hey," he said, beginning to take pity on her. "Where is all this doubt coming from? You've said from the beginning that this is your thing."

"It is, but…"

He nudged her elbow. "Why did you pick this as the menu?"

She picked at her salad without eating. "Well, I tried to come up with something that was fancy enough for a wedding, something special, while keeping in mind the guest list. This is a meal for ranchers and, well, regular people. Not crazy movie stars or visiting dignitaries who only eat fish and sprouted grains or that kind of thing, you know?"

"So you tailored the food to the guest list?"

"Of course. I always do."

"Then why are you so worried? Know what I think? I think that for most people this is going to taste like a fancy meal out that's not intimidating, you know? Nothing they can't recognize or need to pronounce in a foreign language."

Their salads were removed and the main course put in front of them. Rhys's stomach growled. He'd only managed a few bites of the salad and the beef smelled delicious.

"I swear I'm not usually like this. Not so insecure."

"Is it because it's Callum?"

"Maybe. Then again, I don't usually do weddings. That's the one day everyone wants utterly perfect. There's more freedom with parties. But wedding days?" She took another sip of wine. Was quiet for a moment. "I screwed one up once."

"You did?" Was Taylor actually going to admit she'd made a mistake? It didn't strike him as her style.

She nodded. "The bride was allergic to strawberries. I'd forgotten. You don't mess with a bride on her wedding day, you know? She had a breakfast for her bridal party. I never thought twice about giving the chef dominion over the menu. I trusted him completely." She winced at the memory. "The wedding colors were pink and cream. The chef added strawberry coulis to the pancake batter. She got hives and her face swelled up like a balloon. Four hours before her walk down the aisle."

Rhys was intrigued. "What did you do?"

"We tried cold cloths, creams…it wasn't until the antihistamine shot that she really started to improve. But the 'getting ready' photos never happened, and she still looked rather pink and puffy in the pictures. Not to mention the fact that she nodded off in the limousine on the way to the hotel and reception because the drug made her drowsy. Not my finest moment as an event planner."

She speared her golden-browned potatoes with a somewhat savage poke. "I'm telling you, Rhys, you do not mess with a bride on her wedding day."

She looked so fierce he nearly smiled. But there was something else in her expression, too. She didn't like failure, or anything that would reveal a chink in her perfect armor. He wondered why.

"Have you always been a perfectionist?"

She didn't even take it as a slight criticism. "Yes."

"And doesn't that stress you out?"

She shrugged. "Occasionally. As long as I stay organized I'm fine. And I do work best under pressure. It's just now and again something will crop up and I'll chew antacids for a few days."

He wanted to ask her how that could possibly be fun, but they were interrupted as the speeches began. Mr. Shepard welcomed Avery to the family, and then Avery and Callum stood to speak together, thanking their family and friends. They took a moment to thank Taylor for pulling it all together, and Rhys saw her relax a little in her chair. The day was nearly done. The ceremony had gone without a hitch; the reception was lovely and the food delicious. Perhaps she could actually enjoy herself a little during the dancing.

Dessert was served—pastry baskets filled with chocolate mousse and topped with berries and whipped cream. They were almost too pretty to eat, and Rhys noticed that Taylor had slowed down on the wine and accepted a cup of coffee instead.

He frowned. He shouldn't care. Shouldn't bother him that she was wound tighter than a spring or that she was so deliberate in each choice and move. Except he knew now. He knew that there was a vulnerable side. He'd seen it last night when he'd mentioned how her family had ignored her. Whether she acknowledged it or not, she was desperate for her family's approval.

And he knew there was an unpredictable side to her, too, that rarely had a chance to get out to play. Because he was pretty sure that the heavy kissing they'd been doing in the cab of his truck last night had not been planned out and put on a list of pros and cons. It had been spontaneous. And combustible.

When the meal ended, the wedding cake was rolled in. "Oh, it's stunning," Taylor gasped, leaning forward to see better.

"You didn't know? A detail escaped your notice?"

She laughed. "No one was allowed to see it. Avery's friend Denise did it as a wedding gift. Avery insisted I trust her on this and so I did."

"It bothered you, though, right?"

She tore her gaze away from the cake and slid it up to meet his. "A little," she admitted. "This whole experience has been weird. I've had to give up way more control than I normally do. Usually no detail ever escapes my approval."

"Sometimes it's good to let someone else take the reins."

She chuckled. "Not my style, Bullock."

The cake really was pretty, even Rhys could see that. It looked like three presents stacked on top of each other, each layer turned on a slight angle and alternating red and white. The topper looked like a giant red bow. "What's the bow made out of?" he asked Taylor.

"Fondant," she said, smiling. "Okay, so the only thing to worry about now is the music, and the DJ should be fine, so maybe you're right. Maybe I can relax." She sighed. "And finally get some sleep."

He wondered if her lack of sleep was to do with the wedding or if she'd been like him last night, staring at the ceiling wondering what it would have been like to finish what they'd started.

It had been a long time since he'd come that close. He

certainly hadn't wanted to sow any wild oats here in Cadence Creek. The town was too small. Things got around. And before he knew it he'd be tied down, worrying about what he had to offer a wife, wondering how long it would be before he disappointed her.

No danger of that with Taylor, was there? She wasn't staying long enough for that.

Cheers went up as Avery and Callum sliced into the cake. Nell, clearly exhausted, was curled up in Mrs. Shepard's arms, sound asleep. The wait staff cleaned away the remaining dishes and business at the bar picked up. The show was over. Now it was time for fun.

He looked over at Taylor, who was more relaxed but looking increasingly exhausted. He was starting to wonder if she knew what fun was—or if it was all work and no play with her.

She wasn't sure how much more she could take.

Rhys was beside her every moment. He smelled so good. Like those peel-away cologne ads in magazines only better, because the scent came alive from the contact with his warm skin. He knew how to push her buttons and she'd started to realize he did it intentionally, trying to get a rise out of her. It was sexy as all get-out, like a strange mating dance that sent her heart racing and blood to her cheeks.

Which was all well and good except she kept feeling her control slipping and the balance of power was not in her favor. She found herself admitting things that she'd normally never dare breathe. Like that wedding story. She never shared that. It was too humiliating! At least she'd stopped before she'd said anything about how that day had ended—with John walking out. Professional and personal failure in one twelve-hour period. Talk about overachieving…

She didn't quite know where she stood with Rhys. It was partly exhilarating and mostly maddening and now, at the end of a very long day, she was feeling a bit off her game.

She decided to take a few minutes to chill out. She'd done her job. Everyone was doing theirs. It would be okay to relax for a bit. Especially when she could watch her brother and brand-new sister-in-law take to the dance floor for their first waltz.

Rhys disappeared momentarily to the bar and she let out a breath. Avery and Callum swept across the parquet as everyone watched, but her gaze slipped away from the floor and to Rhys, who stood chatting to the bartender while he waited for his drink. She swallowed. His tux fit him to perfection, the trousers showcasing long, lean legs that led to a gorgeously tight bottom. He'd taken off the jacket, and the tailored vest over the white starched shirt accentuated the breadth of his shoulders. He wasn't classically handsome, but his physique was as close to perfect as she could imagine.

When he turned back from the bar he caught her staring. She gasped a little as heat snapped between them, even from across the room. Maybe his face would never be in a magazine, but there was an intensity to it, a magnetism, that she couldn't deny.

He was holding two glasses in his hands.

When he got back to the table, he held one out to her. "Here," he said, taking his seat. "You look like you could use this."

"Champagne?"

He grinned, and it lit her up from the inside. "They managed to have a couple of bottles back there."

"You're more of a beer guy."

"It depends on the occasion. And you—" his gaze traveled over her for about the tenth time today "—look like a girl who needs champagne in her hand."

She took the glass.

"To a job well done."

She raised her glass to touch his but he wasn't done.

"And some well-deserved R&R."

That's right. After tonight she was on vacation for a whole week. She wasn't sure if it was a blessing or if it was going to drive her stir-crazy. She wasn't used to being idle.

She sipped at the champagne, the bubbles exploding on her tongue. A waitress stopped at the table, offering small pieces of cake. What the heck. Taylor took one, and so did Rhys. She took a bite. Not straight up chocolate… She closed her eyes. It was lavender. "Holy cannoli," she whispered, taking another sip of champagne, which only intensified the flavors on her tongue. "That is some serious cake."

"You," he said in a low voice, "are killing me here."

She held his gaze. Put a bit of cake on her fork and held it out while the events of the previous night leaped to the front of her mind. "What's good for the goose," she said lightly, offering the cake. "I promise you, this cake is a life-altering experience."

He took it from the fork. "I don't think it's the cake," he answered, reaching out and circling her wrist with his fingers. "Taylor, what are we doing?"

Clapping erupted as Avery and Callum finished their dance. "Now could we have the wedding party on the floor, please?" the DJ called.

Their gazes clung for a brief second as the words sunk in. For all her "you don't have to act like we're a couple" bit, the truth was they *had* been seated together for the reception and they *were* expected to dance together. The other bridesmaids and groomsmen seated along the head table were getting up from their chairs. Rhys held out his hand. "That's our cue."

She put down her fork. For heaven's sake, it was one dance at a wedding. Nothing to get in such a lather over. She'd put her hand in his, the other on his shoulder, and stare at the buttons on his shirt. It would be fine.

Except the moment they hit the parquet, he pulled her close in his arms and the scent that had teased her earlier enveloped her in a cloud of masculinity. Even in her heels—and she wasn't a short girl—he had a few inches on her. His palm was wide and warm and her plan to simply put her other hand on his lapel was a total fail because she remembered he'd removed his jacket and the flat of her hand was pressed simply to his white shirt. And the hard, warm wall of muscle beneath it.

"For goodness' sake, smile," he commanded as their feet started moving to the music.

She looked up into his eyes. He was smiling down at her but rather than feeling reassured she got the feeling that she was looking into the face of the Big Bad Wolf.

CHAPTER SIX

WHOEVER DECIDED THAT slow, angsty songs were appropriate for weddings needed to be shot.

Taylor made her feet move, determined to keep her distance from Rhys as best she could, which was a rather daunting task considering they were slow dancing. It might have been easier if the song choice had been a wedding standard, something she was used to hearing time and again over the years and could dismiss as cliché and trite. But this was something new and romantic, and an acoustic version to boot that only added to the intimacy. Rhys's hand rode the small of her back, fitting perfectly in the hollow just below the end of her zip. The warmth of his touch seeped through the lace and satin to her skin.

During the planning, a wedding party dance had sounded nice. Since Avery didn't have any family, the traditional Groom/Mom of the Bride, Bride/Father of the Groom dances couldn't happen for the second dance of the night. This was Avery's idea of including everyone. Little had Taylor known that something so innocuous sounding would create such havoc.

"This isn't so bad, is it?"

His breath tickled the hair just above her ear and goose bumps popped up over her skin. How could she say how she really felt about it? That it was pure torture being in his arms this way, determined not to touch, wanting to desperately, knowing she couldn't with such an audience watching their every move?

"Not so bad I guess," she answered.

More shuffling steps. Was she imagining it or did his hand tighten against her back, pulling her closer? She swallowed heavily, the nerves in her stomach swirling with both anxiety and anticipation. Oh, God, now his jaw was resting lightly against her temple and his steps were getting smaller.

Her fingers slid over his shoulders as she imagined the smooth, muscled skin beneath the pure white fabric. Each breath caught for just a moment in her chest, making it hard to breathe as the song went on interminably. His fingers kneaded gently at the precise spot of the dimple at the top of her...

They had to stop this. And yet she lacked any will to back away, to put space between them. What she really wanted was to tilt her head so that his jaw wasn't riding her temple but closer to her mouth.

Holy Hannah.

"What are you doing to me, Taylor?"

If he kept talking in that husky voice she was going to have a meltdown right here on the dance floor.

"Nothing," she replied. "I'm not doing anything."

But she was and she knew it. And he wasn't exactly backing off, either.

"You..." Fear crowded her breath. She was getting in way too deep. "You don't even like me. You criticize everything."

"You're not the only one who enjoys a challenge," he replied, his thumb making circles against her tailbone. "You know as well as I do all that baiting was just foreplay."

Melt. Down.

"You're forgetting," he said softly, "who was with you in that truck last night."

She finally braved a look at him. His dark eyes glittered at her and she knew in a heartbeat where this would lead if she let it. The big question was did she want to?

Her body said yes. Her brain was another matter entirely. And while it was a close-fought battle, her brain was still in charge. By a very narrow margin.

"Not going to happen," she said, sounding far more certain than she felt.

"You sure? No gravel pit required. I have my own house, with a nice big bed in it."

Oh. *Oh.*

While that was a temptingly delicious thought, Taylor knew one of them had to be sensible. "I haven't had that much champagne, Rhys. If you're looking to hook up with someone, maybe you can find someone local. I'm sure there are some pretty girls in town who'd be interested."

He lifted his chin and his hot gaze slid away. "I don't date town girls."

"Ever?"

"Ever," he confirmed tightly.

Well. There was a story there, she was sure. But she wasn't about to ask. The farther away from Rhys she could manage the better. She did not want to get involved. A couple of stolen kisses were one thing. Start to probe into his personal life and it was going to get intimate.

"So I'm what? Not hanging around after Christmas, which makes me convenient?"

He let out a short laugh, dropped his gaze to her lips and pulled her close. Her breath came out in a rush as she found herself pressed against his hard length. "Trust me. You are anything but convenient."

The contact rippled through them both until suddenly

he released his hold and stepped back. The song ended and a new one began. Other guests crowded the floor as a popular, upbeat song thumped through the speakers.

Taylor stepped back. "Thank you for the dance."

Before he could say anything else, she turned her back on him and went to their table, ready to pick up her purse and go. Except she hadn't brought a vehicle, had she? She'd gone to the church in the limo and to here with Rhys and now she'd have to beg a ride back to the B&B. Which she'd planned to do with Jack, but she caught sight of him dancing with Amy Wilson, having a good time.

She grabbed her champagne glass and drained what was in it.

Callum and Avery stopped for a moment, happy and glowing. "Taylor, we can't thank you enough," Avery said. "Today was just perfect."

She was relieved to have something to think about other than Rhys. "It was my pleasure. And I did have some help you know. Your florist is a gem and your cake was out of this world. Not to mention Clara saving the day with the church candles." She looked up at Callum. "You've landed in a very nice place, brother."

He winked at her. "I know it. Sure you don't want to hang around a little longer?"

She shook her head. "A nice diversion but not my style. The week of relaxation that I'll get housesitting for you is enough small-town for me, thanks."

"You sure? Seems to me you've made a friend." He raised his eyebrows.

"I'm a big girl. And that's going nowhere, so don't you worry your head about it."

"That's not what Jack says. He said you were necking with Rhys in his truck last night."

This was what she didn't miss about having brothers

underfoot. They always thought it was okay to stick their noses in her business under the guise of "looking out for their sister." All of it was a pain in the butt.

"Callum," Avery chided softly, elbowing her husband in the ribs.

"Well, they weren't exactly discreet on the dance floor, either."

Taylor's cheeks burned. "Rhys Bullock is a bossy so-and-so who likes to push my buttons. I'm no more interested in him than...than..."

A hand appeared beside her, reaching for the other champagne glass. She turned on him. "Could you please stop showing up everywhere I am?"

He lifted his glass in a mock toast, totally unperturbed. "I'll disappear somewhere more convenient," he said.

He did, too. Right back to the dance floor. The DJ had put on a faster number and Rhys snagged Amy from Jack and swung her into a two-step. He turned her under his arm and she came back laughing.

"You're jealous," Callum noted.

"I most certainly am not."

"You're no better at lying now than you were when we were kids. Dad always said the poker face gene passed you by." Callum grinned, but he couldn't possibly know how much the words stung. Another criticism. She never measured up. She was always one step behind her brothers as far as her dad was concerned. One of these days she was going to show her father her accounts and watch his eyebrows go up. Those "frivolous" parties she planned brought in a boatload of cash.

Funny how the idea of that future moment had always seemed so sweet in her mind, but lately it had lost a little of its lustre. It was only a bank statement after all. There had to be more, right? Something more satisfying than the account balance?

"Don't you have cows to milk or something?"

He laughed. "I hired someone to do that today." His eyes twinkled at her. "And you won't have to worry about any farm work, either, while you're at the house. It's all taken care of."

"Good. Because you used to enjoy mucking around in the barns but I'd rather keep my boots nice and clean."

He laughed, then leaned forward and kissed her cheek. "We'll be gone tomorrow before you get to the house. I'll leave the key under the Santa by the door. Make yourself at home and we'll see you on the twenty-third."

She relaxed and kissed him back. "Love you, Callum."

"I love you, too, brat."

They moved off to visit with other guests. Taylor took a turn on the floor with Ty, and Sam, and even once with her father. True to form, he complimented the wedding but in such a way that it made her feel inconsequential.

"You planned a nice little party," he said, smiling at her.

Her throat tightened. Eighty guests, wedding party, church, venue, catering, flowers and all the other tiny details it took to put a wedding together in a ridiculously short amount of time. And it was "little"?

"Thanks," she said, deflated but unwilling to rise to any bait tonight. Not on Callum's day.

"When are you going to stop playing and start putting that business degree to good use?" he asked.

"I am putting my degree to use," she returned, moving automatically to the music. "Just ask my accountant."

"Planning parties?"

"I know you've never understood that. You wanted me to be a fund manager. I'd be bored to death, Dad."

She made herself look into his face as she said it. For

a moment he'd almost looked hurt. How was that even possible?

Conversation dropped for a minute or so before Harry recovered and changed the subject, talking nonstop about Nell and how it was wonderful to have a grandchild to spoil. The dance ended just in time—she was starting to worry he was going to ask her when she was going to do her duty and provide some more grandchildren. Her father's opinions were clear enough and pretty much paralleled with what John's had been. Personal and professional failure. And if not failure, at the least disappointment.

When the dance was over Rhys gave her a wide berth and she attempted to perk up her mood by spending a half hour with the pregnant Clara, chatting about Angela's charity foundation Butterfly House, and the other initiatives the Diamonds were involved in. It was all quite fascinating and before she knew it, the call went up for the single women to gather on the floor for the throwing of the bouquet.

She was not going to do that. Not in a million years.

Except Avery put up the call and every eye was on her. "Come on, Taylor, you, too!" Taylor spied Rhys standing against a pillar, his arms folded smugly as his eyes teased her, daring her to take part in the silly custom. She lifted her chin and ran her hands down her skirt before joining the half-dozen or so women ready to do battle for the mythical status of the next to be married. She wouldn't give him the satisfaction of backing out. Not that she'd actively try to catch it...

When Avery let the bouquet fly, Taylor had a heart-stopping moment when she realized it was heading right for her. Without thinking she simply reacted, raising her hands. But just before the ribbon-wrapped stems reached her, another hand neatly plucked it from the air.

Cheers went up when Amy Wilson held up the bouquet in a sign of victory.

Taylor was really ready to leave now. As she backed off the dance floor, she looked over at her mother, smiling from the sidelines, still cradling a sleeping Nell in her arms. Taylor wondered if her mom knew how much Taylor admired her. It was always her dad in the spotlight, but Taylor knew how hard her mom worked to keep the ship on course. Once, when she'd been about ten years old, she'd discovered her mother in the kitchen, making lists for an upcoming party they were hosting. That was when Taylor understood how, when everything seemed smooth and effortless on the surface, it was because of a well-oiled, well-organized machine running things behind the scenes. The machine, in that case, had been her mother, who handled everything from start to finish and still found time to run the kids to sports and especially Jack to his ski meets.

Maybe her dad was the one with his picture in the business magazines, but it was her mother Taylor truly admired. Her mother was the reason she'd chosen event planning as her career. Taylor hated how her father minimized the hard work she did, so why did her mother not resent his attitude? Why had it never been an issue for them?

There was another loud shout and Taylor lifted her head to see a stunned Rhys holding the bridal garter. According to tradition, Amy then took the chair in the middle of the dance floor while Rhys slid the garter on her leg. Taylor stifled a laugh. He didn't look too happy about it, especially when the DJ announced that the next dance was for the "lucky couple." Served him right.

As the music started, she headed toward her parents. "I don't suppose you're heading back to the B&B anytime soon, are you?" she asked, kneeling by her mom's chair.

"As a matter of fact, I was just suggesting to your dad

that we should take Nell and go. She's staying with us to-night so Callum and Avery can have the place to them-selves before they all fly out tomorrow. Poor little mite's had enough excitement for today."

"So has this big mite. I'm beat. Mind if I catch a lift?"

"Of course not, but don't you want to stay at the party?"

Taylor saw Rhys and Amy out of the corner of her eye. For all he said he didn't date local girls, Amy sure was snuggled close to him, her arms wrapped around his ribs and her head nestled into his shoulder. "I'm sure. I've had a long few days and this will pretty much run itself now."

"Get your things then. You did a beautiful job, sweet-heart. Proud of you."

The words warmed Taylor's heart. "Thanks, Mom. I had a good teacher."

"Oh, go on."

But Taylor took a moment to press her mother's hand in hers. "I mean it. I don't know that you were appreciated enough for all you did to keep things running smoothly. I should have said this before, but when I started my busi-ness you were the inspiration behind it."

"I didn't know that."

"Well, it's true."

Taylor went to pull away but her mom held tight to her hand. "Mind if I give you a little extra food for thought?"

Surprised, Taylor paused. "Sure."

Susan looked into Taylor's eyes and smiled. "None of it would have meant a thing without your dad and you kids. I know sometimes it looked like I played the dutiful wife…"

"You worked hard."

"Yes, I did, and I enjoyed it. Still, I would have missed out on so much if I hadn't had you kids. I could have gone on and done anything I wanted, you know? And I don't regret my decision for a second. Work is work, but family is forever."

"Didn't it ever bother you that Dad, well, took you for granted?"

Susan laughed. "Is that what you think? Oh, heavens. He wanted you kids, too. Honey, you get so wound up and defensive about this division of labor expectation, but it goes both ways. We did what worked for us. Being home with you three was my choice to make."

"Is this leading to a speech about settling down?"

Susan smiled and patted her hand. "I know better than that."

Taylor let out a breath. "Phew." But after a moment she looked at her mother again. "Mom, maybe I will settle down. When I find the right guy."

"That's a good answer," her mother replied. "Now, let's get going. I want to spend a little more time with my new granddaughter tonight."

Taylor got her coat from the coat check, snagged her purse and checked in with the staff one last time. Her mother was making sure they had all of Nell's stuff—including her car seat—while her dad went to warm up the car. She was just pulling on her gloves when Rhys came up behind her.

"You were just going to leave without saying goodbye?"

She held on to her purse strap. "It's been a long day and I'm catching a ride with my folks."

"That didn't answer my question."

She frowned. "What do you care? You've amused yourself with me a bit for the last few days but the wedding's over, we're not paired up anymore and we can both go about our business."

Rhys stared at her quizzically. "Really?"

"Is there some reason why we shouldn't?"

He looked like he wanted to say something, but held back. She wondered why. And then got a bit annoyed that she kept wondering about Rhys's state of mind at all. She blew air out her nose in an exasperated huff. "What do you care anyway? You seemed to enjoy having Amy Wilson plastered all over you."

"Jealous?"

She snorted. "Hardly."

He stepped forward until there was barely an inch between them. "Amy Wilson is the last woman on earth I want to be with!"

Silence rang around them, and then, almost as one, they realized someone had heard the entire outburst. Amy stood not ten feet away, her creamy skin stained crimson in embarrassment as humiliated tears shone in her eyes.

"Amy…" Taylor tried, taking a hesitant step toward the woman.

But Amy lifted a hand to halt Taylor's progress, and without saying a word she spun on her heel and disappeared into the women's powder room.

Rhys sighed heavily, let out a breathy expletive.

"Good night, Rhys."

"Taylor, I'm…"

But she didn't listen to the end. She turned and walked, quickly, toward the exit. She could see the headlights of her dad's rental car as it waited by the front door, saw him helping her mom in the passenger side. She went outside and was met by a frigid wall of arctic air. As she climbed into the backseat, she made a promise to herself.

Tomorrow she was going to stock up on groceries, wine and DVDs. Then she was going to go to Callum's house and as God as her witness, she wasn't going to venture out into the icy cold for the entire week. She was going to be a hermit. No work. No worrying about freezing her tail off.

And especially no men!

CHAPTER SEVEN

TAYLOR ROLLED OVER and squinted at the sunshine coming through the bedroom window. Why hadn't she thought to close the blinds last night? Her first full day of vacation and she'd looked forward to sleeping in. She checked her watch. It was only eight-fifteen!

She burrowed into the warm blankets and closed her eyes. Maybe if she breathed deeply and relaxed, she could fall back asleep. But after just a few minutes she knew she might as well get up. She was awake for good now. Besides, just because she was up didn't mean she had to actually "do" anything. She could lounge around in her fuzzy pajamas, drink coffee, read one of the paperbacks she'd brought along.

Come to think of it, that sounded pretty darn good. Especially the coffee part. It was going to be awesome having some peace and quiet. No ringing phones, no buzzing email, no wedding plans and especially no Rhys Bullock to get in her way now that the wedding was over.

She was terribly afraid she was going to be bored to tears within forty-eight hours.

She rolled out of bed and shoved her feet into her favorite sheepskin slippers. On the way to the kitchen she pulled her hair back into a messy ponytail, anchoring it with a hair elastic that had been left on her wrist. While the coffee was brewing she turned up the thermostat and chafed her arms. Even the soft fleece of her winter PJs was no protection against the December cold.

She poured her first cup of coffee and, in keeping with the celebratory nature of the week, substituted her usual cream with the festive eggnog she found in the refrigerator.

She was halfway through the cup when she chanced a look out the front window. The mug paused inches away from her lips as she stared at a familiar brown truck. What on earth was Rhys doing here?

As she stared, the man in question came out of the barn. Even with the hat pulled low over his head, she'd recognize that long-legged stride in a heartbeat.

Irritation marred her idyllic morning and before she could think twice she flung open the door and stepped to the threshold. "What on earth are you doing here?"

His head snapped up and even though he was too far away for her to see his eyes, she felt the connection straight to her toes. Stupid girl. She should have stayed inside. Pretended she wasn't home. Not risen to the bait, except Rhys seemed to get on her last nerve without trying. She swallowed thickly, feeling quite foolish but standing her ground as a matter of pride. He hadn't actually baited her at all. He hadn't done *anything*.

Except show up.

"Well?" she persisted.

"I'm doing the chores." His tone said, *What does it look like I'm doing?*

She frowned. Callum had said at the reception that someone had looked after the chores and would continue to do so during his absence. He couldn't have meant Rhys. Rhys had been occupied with the wedding all day on Saturday. She would have noticed if he'd slipped away.

"Why?"

He came closer, walking across the yard as if he owned the damned place. "Well, I would suppose that would be because Callum hired me to."

"He did not. He hired someone else."

Rhys was only twenty feet away now. "He told you that?"

The wrinkle between her eyebrows deepened. Was that exactly what Callum had said? "He said he hired someone to do the chores during the wedding and during his absence, too."

Rhys stopped at the bottom of the steps to the veranda. "He hired Keith O'Brien on the day of the wedding, because I was in the wedding party."

Oh, hell.

"Why didn't he just hire him for the whole time, then?" She gave a huff that went up in a cloud of frosty air.

"Because Keith left yesterday to go to Fort McMurray to spend the holidays with his family."

"So you're..."

He shifted his weight to one hip, a move that made him look unbearably cocky. "Here for the week," he finished for her, his whole stance screaming *deal with it*.

And then he smiled, that slow grin climbing up his cheek that was at once maddening and somehow, at the same time, made her whole body go warm. His gaze slid over her pajamas. "Penguins? Seriously?" he asked.

Her mouth dropped open as she realized she was standing in the doorway still in her nightwear. Jolly skiing penguins danced down the light blue pant legs. The navy fleece top was plain except for one more penguin on the left breast.

She stepped back inside and slammed the door.

It was eerily quiet for the space of five seconds, and

then her heart beat with the sound of his boots, heavy on the steps, then two more as he crossed the narrow porch.

He was just on the other side of the door. Less than two feet away. He didn't even have the manners to knock. It was like he knew she was standing there waiting for him because he said, in a low voice, "Aren't you going to ask me in for coffee?"

"Humph!" she huffed, taking a step backward and fuming, her hands on her hips. As if. Presumptuous jerk!

"Come on, Taylor. It's cold out here. A man could use a hot cup of joe. I can smell it, for Pete's sake."

"I hear the coffee is good at the Wagon Wheel. Price is right, too."

Was that a chuckle she heard or had she just imagined it?

Softer now, he answered, "But the company isn't nearly as good."

She shouldn't be persuaded or softening toward him at all. He was used to getting his own way and she wouldn't oblige.

Then he said the words she never thought he'd ever utter. "I'm sorry about the other night."

Damn him.

She opened the door. "Come in then, before you let all the heat out. It's like an igloo in here."

He stepped inside, all six-feet-plus of him, even taller with his Stetson on. She wasn't used to seeing him this way—he looked like the real deal with his boots and hat and heavy jacket.

"You smell like the barn."

"My grandfather would say that's the smell of money."

"Money?"

He grinned. "Yeah. Anyway, sorry. Occupational hazard. Me smelling like the animals, that is. Though usually I smell like horses. They smell better than cows."

She didn't actually mind. While she wasn't interested in getting her own boots dirty, she did remember days on her uncle's farm. The smell was familiar and not too unpleasant.

"Just take off your boots if you're coming in for coffee."

While he toed off his boots she went into the kitchen to get a fresh cup. "What do you take in it?" she called out.

"Just cream, if you've got it," he answered, stepping inside the sunny kitchen.

She handed him the cup and then took a plastic container from a cupboard. "Are you hungry? Avery left a mountain of food, way more than I can eat in a week. This one is chocolate banana bread."

"I couldn't turn that down."

She cut several slices and put them on a plate. "Come on and sit down then."

Before Rhys sat down, he removed his hat and put it carefully on a nearby stool. She stared at him as he sat, pulled his chair in and reached for his coffee cup.

"What?" he asked, pausing with the cup halfway to his lips.

She shrugged. "You can be very annoying. But you have very good manners."

He laughed. "Blame my mom, I guess. So, enjoying your vacation?"

"Well, I've only officially been on holiday for a few hours. Yesterday I slept in, then spent last night hanging with my family. My mom and dad booked a place in Radium for the week and are coming back on the twenty-third for Christmas with Callum and the family. And Jack flew back to Montana this morning for a meeting of some sort. Lord only knows what deal he's cooking up this time.

Anyway, I'll probably enjoy my vacation for a few days. And then I'll start going stir-crazy."

Rhys reached for a slice of cake. "You strike me as one of those ambitious, type A personality people."

"You mean I'm driven? Yeah, I guess." She sighed. "I might as well 'fess up. I like being my own boss. Sometimes it's stressful because it's all on me, you know? But I don't like being told what to do."

He began coughing, crumbs catching in his throat. When he looked up at her again his eyes had watered and he was laughing. "Sorry. Stating the obvious shouldn't have been that funny."

"Hey, I know how you feel about it. You think I'm crazy. Most guys are intimidated by it."

"Most guys have a hard time with a woman who is smarter than they are."

She nibbled on her cake. "Careful, Rhys. That almost sounded like a compliment."

He laughed.

"So why aren't you?"

"What?" He tilted his head curiously. "What do you mean?"

"Why aren't you intimidated?"

He smiled again and the dark depths of his eyes warmed. "Oh. That's easy. I said that most guys have a problem with women who are smarter than they are..."

"And you're not most guys?"

"I never said you were smarter than me."

Without thinking, she kicked him under the table. Her toe hurt but he barely even flinched. "You are an infernal tease!"

"And you love it. Because you like a challenge."

How did he possibly know her so well? It was vastly unsettling.

She picked at her cake another moment or two before putting it down and facing him squarely. "What do you get out of this, Rhys? You and me. We're doing this dance and I'm not sure I see the point of it."

"You mean because we're so different and all?"

She lifted one shoulder. "That's only part of it. We both know that on Boxing Day I'm headed back to my life, so why bother?"

Taylor lifted her gaze to meet his. Something curled through her insides, hot and exciting. This simmering attraction they had going on made no sense. They were as different as water and air. But it was there just the same. This chemistry. Rhys Bullock was exciting. A small-town farmworker who hadn't the least bit of initiative and she couldn't stop thinking about him.

And yet, maybe the attraction stemmed from his confidence, a self-assurance that he knew who he was and was exactly where he wanted to be. While she didn't quite understand his choices, she had to admit she was the tiniest bit jealous that he'd gained that understanding while she was still trying to figure it all out. He didn't need accolades. Rhys Bullock had the confidence to know exactly who he was. He was comfortable in his own skin the way she'd never been.

"Why you?" He leaned forward a little. "Beyond the obvious fact that you're crazy hot and my temperature goes up a few degrees when you enter the room?"

She suppressed the urge to fan herself. "Rhys," she cautioned.

"You asked. And for what it's worth, I'm not looking for ties and commitments."

"Funny, because you're a pretty grounded guy. I'd kind of expect someone like you to be settled down with two-point-five kids and a dog, you know?"

Something flickered across his face. Pain? Anger? It disappeared as fast as it had arrived. "Start dating in a town this size and suddenly the town gets very, very small. Especially when things go wrong."

"Ah, like that old saying about…doing something where you eat."

He chuckled. "Yeah. Exactly like that. Look, you're a novelty, Taylor. An adventure. A safe one, because in a week's time you're going to be gone."

"So I'm a fling?"

His gaze sharpened. "A couple of kisses hardly constitutes a fling." He took a calm sip of his coffee. "You're an anomaly. You intrigue me. You know how to keep me on my toes."

"I'm glad I'm so amusing."

"Don't act like your feelings are hurt. We both know that the last thing you want is to be ordinary."

"Yeah, well, not everyone appreciates the alternative."

"That's because you highlight every single one of their flaws. You're not always right, but you're committed." He put his hand over hers. "That kind of commitment can take a toll. I can see you need the break."

"Don't be silly. I'm perfectly fine." She looked away, unexpectedly touched by his insight. How could he see what everyone else did not? The whole wedding she'd felt like she was losing her edge. Normally she'd be fired up and excited about the New Year's job, but instead she was dreading it. What on earth was wrong with her?

He squeezed her fingers. "Oh, Taylor, do you think I don't recognize burnout when I see it?"

She pulled her hand out of his grasp and sat back. "I'm not even thirty years old. I'm too young for burnout. Besides, what would you know about the pressures of running a business, with your 'put in your shift and go home' attitude?"

Silence rang in the kitchen for a few seconds. "Okay then." He pushed out the chair, stood and reached for his hat. "I should get going. I have some work out at Diamondback before coming back tonight to do the evening chores. Thanks for the coffee and cake."

She felt silly for going off on him like that—especially when he was right. At the same time, she didn't need to have it pointed out so bluntly. And the way he'd spoken so softly and squeezed her fingers? Argh! The sympathy had made her both angry and inexplicably tearful.

"Rhys, I…"

"Don't worry about it," he said evenly, going to the door and pulling on his boots. "I'll see you later."

He was gone before she had a chance to do anything. To take back the snippy words. She'd judged him, when she knew how it felt to be on the receiving end of such judgment.

She turned her back to the door and leaned against it, staring at the Christmas tree, fully decorated, standing in the corner. She couldn't even muster up a good dose of Christmas cheer.

Maybe Rhys was right. Maybe she was a little burned out. But she couldn't just take off and leave things. She had clients and commitments. She had employees who were counting on her for their livelihoods.

One week. Somehow she needed to recharge during this one week. With a heavy sigh, she went to the kitchen, retrieved her coffee and headed back to the bedroom. Coffee and a book in bed was as good a start as she could come up with right now.

Rhys was glad of the physical labor to keep him going. He'd been up early to head to Callum's for chores, then to

Diamondback, and now back at Callum's for the evening milking. Plus he hadn't been sleeping well. He'd had Taylor on his mind. Something had happened between them as they'd danced at the wedding. Then there was this morning in the kitchen. Lord, how he loved bantering with her. She was quick and sharp and it was like a mating dance, teasing then pulling away. Except that when it got a little too honest she ran scared and the game was over.

It was fully dark outside as he finished tidying the milking parlor and went to the stainless sink to wash his hands. What was she doing now? Having dinner? A bubble bath? His fingers paused for a moment as that idea saturated his consciousness, crowding out any other thoughts. He imagined her long, pale limbs slick with water and soap, tendrils of hair curling around her face from the steam rising from the bath.

Not dating came with a price. It was like anything else, he supposed. Deny yourself long enough, and temptation was nearly too much to bear. And Taylor Shepard was tempting indeed.

But he knew what she really thought of him. That fact alone would keep him from knocking on her door again.

He shut off the tap. He knew a damn sight more about running a business than she thought. His livelihood and his mother's future were tied up in the diner. And he knew the pain of failure, too. It wasn't even a matter of his savings. It was a matter of trying to make things right for employees. Creditors. Putting himself last, and scraping the bottom of the barrel to keep from declaring bankruptcy. The unfortunate part was that he hadn't just messed things up for himself. It had messed up Sherry's life. And by extension, that of her kids.

He rubbed a hand over his face.

Never again. Punching a clock made for a lot less stress in the end. Taylor had no right to judge him for it.

He shoved his gloves on his hands and stepped outside into the cold. His feet crunched on the snow and he was nearly to his truck when the front door to the house opened.

"Rhys?"

He turned. His breath formed a frosty cloud as he saw her standing in the circle of porch light, her arms crossed around her middle to keep warm. Her long braid fell over her shoulder again, neat and tidy. Just once he'd like to take that braid apart with his fingers and sink his hands into the thick softness of her hair.

"You need something?" he called out.

There was a slight hesitation. "I… Do you want to come in for a few minutes?"

Hell, yes. Which was exactly why he shouldn't.

"It's been a long day, Taylor." He put his hand on the door handle.

"Oh."

That was all she said. Oh. But he was just stupid enough to hear disappointment in her voice as well as a recognition that it wasn't about the long day at all.

He closed his eyes briefly. This was very likely going to be a big mistake. Huge.

"Maybe just for a minute."

She waited for him, though she had to be nearly freezing by now. She stepped aside as he climbed the steps and went inside to where it was warm. He heard the door shut behind him and fought the urge to turn and kiss her. The desire to take her in his arms was so strong it was nearly overwhelming. Whatever differences they had, the connection between them was undeniable. It made things very complicated.

"Did you need something?" he asked. "I'm pretty handy if something needs fixing."

Taylor slid past him into the living room. He noticed now that the tree was lit up, a beautiful specimen glowing with white lights and red and silver decorations. A few presents were beneath it, wrapped in expensive foil paper with precise red and green bows. "Tree looks good."

"Avery did it before she left."

"I didn't notice it this morning."

She met his gaze and he'd swear she was shy. "It looks different when it's lit up."

"So do you."

He shouldn't have said it. Keeping his mouth shut had never been much of a problem for him before. But there was nothing usual about Taylor, was there? She provoked all kinds of unexpected responses.

"About this morning," she said quietly. "I asked you in tonight because I owe you an apology."

He didn't know what to say. Taylor didn't strike him as the type who apologized. Or at least—came right out and said it. He recalled the night of the rehearsal dinner, and how Taylor had told Martha that she'd underestimated her. She'd expressed the sentiment in a roundabout way when talking to Rhys. But not a full-on apology.

She came forward and looked up into his eyes. "I was overly sensitive this morning, and I said something I shouldn't have. It's not up to me to judge your life choices. Everyone makes their own decisions for their own reasons and their own happiness. I don't like it when people do it to me, and I shouldn't have done it to you."

He'd respected her intelligence before, admired how capable she was. But this was different. Taylor had a lot of pride. Making a point of saying she was sorry took humility.

"It's a bit of a hot-button with me," he admitted. "I tend to be a bit sensitive about it."

"Why?" She cocked her head a little, and the motion made him smile.

"It's a long and boring story," he said lightly.

"I bet it's not. Which is why you're not talking."

He couldn't help it, he smiled back. It might be easier to stay away if he didn't actually *like* her—but he did. She was straightforward and honest and made him laugh.

"Listen," she said, her voice soft. "I made cannelloni for dinner and there's enough to share. Have you eaten yet?"

Her lips had some sort of gloss on them that didn't add much color but made them look shiny and plump. He swallowed and dragged his gaze from her mouth back to her eyes. "Um, no."

"Take your boots off, then, and come inside. I promise that I won't poison you."

She said it with one eyebrow raised and her lips curved up in good humor.

He questioned the wisdom of hanging around, and then his stomach rumbled. As Taylor laughed, he took off his boots and left them by the door.

"Bathroom's through there, if you want to wash your hands. I'll dish stuff up."

When he arrived back in the kitchen, the scent of tomato and garlic seduced his nostrils. "That smells so good," he commented, pausing in the doorway.

She'd only left on the under-counter lighting, which cast a warm and intimate glow through the room. A cheery red and green plaid tablecloth covered the table, and she'd lit a couple of stubby candles in the middle.

Suddenly he wondered if he'd fallen very neatly into a trap. And if he actually minded so very much.

"Do you eat like this every night?" he asked casually, stepping into the room.

Taylor blushed. "Confession time, I guess. I planned dinner a little late because I was hoping you'd say yes." She placed a glass casserole dish on a hot mat on the table, then added a bowl of salad and a bottle of white wine. "I thought I'd have some wine, but if you'd prefer something else?"

"Wine is fine. Just a single glass, though." He was trying to decide what he felt about her admission that she'd planned dinner with him in mind. "You wanted me to come to dinner, and yet this morning you were pretty mad about seeing me here."

She hesitated, wine bottle in hand. "You complicate things for me. But I was here today at loose ends, no work to do, no one to talk to. It seemed lonely to eat here alone and I didn't want to go into town again."

"So I'm a chair filler."

"I decided to stop being annoyed with you and enjoy your company instead." She finished pouring the wine.

When she was seated he sat, and reached for the cloth napkin. "What do you do in Vancouver, then? I mean, at meal times?"

It occurred to him that maybe she didn't eat dinner alone. A beautiful woman like her. It was stupid to think she wasn't taken, wasn't it?

She took his plate and served him a helping of the stuffed pasta. "I usually pick up something on my way home. Or I get home so late I just grab something quick in front of the TV before hitting the bed."

"This pace must be a real change for you."

"A bit. Different, but not entirely unwelcome, actually."

She added salad to his plate and handed it back. "I'm very good at what I do, Rhys. I've built the business from the ground up and I'm proud of it. But sometimes I do wonder if I'm missing out on something."

He nearly bobbled his plate. "You're joking, right?"

"Not really." She sighed. "Of course, it's entirely possible I just need a vacation. I haven't taken any time off in a while."

"Since when?"

She served herself and picked up her fork. "Nearly three years. I took a very brief four-day trip to Hawaii. A few days of sun, sand and fruity drinks with umbrellas."

"Four days isn't much time."

"It was what I could manage. It's not like punching a clock and putting in for two weeks of holiday time."

"I know that." He tasted his first bite of cannelloni. Flavor exploded on his tongue—rich, creamy cheese, fresh basil, ripe tomatoes. "This is really good, Taylor. I never knew you could cook."

"My mom taught me."

"Your mom? Really? She strikes me as a society wife. Don't take that the wrong way," he warned. "Your mom seems very nice. But I kind of see her as someone who, I don't know, has things catered. Who outsources."

Taylor nodded. "Sometimes. But growing up—we weren't hurting for money, but we didn't have household staff, either. Mom kept us kids in line, helped with homework, decorated like Martha Stewart and cooked for her own dinner parties. At least until we were much older, and Dad's firm was on really solid ground." She speared a leaf of lettuce. "I learned a lot about my event planning biz from my Mom. She's an organizational whiz."

"Hmm," he mused. "Seems we have something in common after all. While my old man was out taking care of business, my mom held down the fort for me and my brother. I've never met another woman who could make something out of nothing. She worked at the diner during the day, but she was always helping my dad with his ventures."

"What did he do?"

Rhys shrugged. "What didn't he do? He sold insurance for a while, a two-man operation here in Cadence Creek. When that didn't fly, he was a sales rep for some office supply company, traveling all around Alberta. He sold used cars after that if I remember right."

And a bunch of other jobs and schemes that had taken him away more than he was home, and never panned out as he'd hoped. Time and again he'd moved on to something newer and shinier, and financially they'd gone further and further in the hole.

"Sounds industrious," Taylor commented easily, reaching for the wine and topping up her glass.

"Yeah, he was a real go-getter," Rhys agreed, trying very hard to keep the bitterness out of his voice and not doing such a great job. He'd loved his dad but the legacy he'd left behind wasn't the greatest.

She put the bottle down carefully and frowned. "You aren't happy about that, are you?"

He focused on his pasta. "Dad was full of bright ideas and a little fuzzier on the execution. It was my mom who kept her feet on the ground and really provided for us kids. Problem was, every time Dad moved on to something better, he usually left some damage in his wake. Debts he couldn't pay and employees out of a job. It didn't get him the greatest goodwill here, you know? We were lucky that everyone loved my mom. Otherwise maybe we would've been run out of Cadence Creek."

"Surely it wasn't that bad," Taylor said, smiling.

"I know I wasn't supposed to hear, but one day I was passing by the hardware store and I heard these guys outside talking. They called him 'Big Man Bullock' and not in a nice way."

He couldn't look at her. For some reason that single memory had shaped him so much more than any other from his childhood, good and bad. In that moment he'd decided he would never be like his father. Never. Only for a while he had been. He'd let so many people down. It was his biggest regret.

"So that's why you don't want to own your own business? You don't want to fail like your dad did?"

Rhys nodded and stabbed some salad with his fork. "That's exactly why. You said it yourself—you're responsible and can't just take off on a whim. You have other people relying on you." His throat tightened and he cleared the lump away. "You mess up and it's other lives you're affecting, not just your own. I would never want anyone to speak about me the way they were speaking about him that day. My brother and I both left home after high school. It was two less mouths for my mom to try to feed, to be honest."

Silence hummed through the kitchen. It hadn't turned out to be a very pleasant conversation after all. All it had done was stir up things he'd rather forget.

"Well," she said softly. "You're back in Cadence Creek now, and the diner is the heart of this town, and your mom is fabulous. You're steady and reliable, Rhys. There are worse things." She patted his hand. "You don't have to live down your father's reputation. That was his, not yours. You came back to help your mom. Not everyone would do that."

She seemed so sure that she said the right thing as she smiled again and turned back to her meal.

Rhys's appetite, though, shriveled away to nothing as he picked at his food. She had no idea, none at all. Yes, he'd come back when his father died because Martha had needed him. And he'd gone against his instincts and done what she'd asked of him because she was his mother and he couldn't stand the thought of disappointing one more person. He wondered what Taylor would say if she knew he'd gone from one bad venture into immediately investing in another?

He'd come back to Cadence Creek with his tail between his legs. He was more like his old man than anyone knew.

And he hated it.

CHAPTER EIGHT

THEY RETIRED TO the living room after dinner. Taylor made coffee and insisted they leave the dishes. She'd need something to keep her busy tomorrow anyway. Besides, Rhys had turned surprisingly quiet. She wondered what that was about.

"You okay?" she asked, offering him a shortbread cookie.

"Sure, why wouldn't I be?" he responded, taking one from the plate.

"I don't know. You got quiet all of a sudden. After we talked about your dad."

She looked over at him. Despite his relaxed pose, his jaw was tight. "Rhys," she said gently, "did you feel like it was your job to look after everyone after he died?"

"Why are we talking about this?" He shoved the cookie in his mouth, the buttery crumbs preventing him from saying more. But Taylor waited. Waited for him to chew and swallow and wash it down with a sip of coffee.

"Because," she finally answered, "it seems to me you could use a friend. And that maybe, since I'm not from Cadence Creek, I might be a logical choice."

Confusion cluttered his eyes as they met hers. "Do I strike you as the confiding type?"

She smiled. "Maybe you could make an exception. This once."

He seemed to debate for a while. Taylor pulled her knees up toward her chin and sank deeper into the cushions of the sofa, cradling her cup in her hands. How long had it been since she'd spent an evening like this, with a warm cuppa in front of a glowing tree? No files open, no cell phone ringing. Just a rugged cowboy and coffee and cookies.

Simple. And maybe it would bore her in a couple of days, but for right now it was quite heavenly.

"I had my own business once," he confided, staring into his cup. "I had an office based in Rocky Mountain House. I'd wanted to start something away from Cadence Creek, away from my dad's reputation. I was determined to make a go of it, the way he'd never been able to."

She got a sinking feeling about where this was headed. "What kind of business?"

"Feed supplements," he said simply. "I had an office, a couple of office staff and a few reps other than myself who traveled the area to the various ranches. For a while it was okay. Then I started losing money. It got to a point where I wasn't even drawing a salary, just so I could pay my staff. I fell behind on the office rent and we shifted it to run from my house."

His face took on a distant look for a few seconds, but then he gave his head a little shake and it cleared. "It wasn't long before I knew I had to shut it down or declare bankruptcy. Since I didn't want the mark on my credit rating, I closed my doors. My final accounts owing paid my back rent and wages and I got a job as a ranch hand. I got to bring home a paycheck while my employees had to file for Employment Insurance since I laid them off. They had families. Little kids. Mortgages."

"But surely they didn't blame you!"

He shrugged, but the distant look was back. "A million times I went over what I might have done differently, to manage it better. The jobs I took—working the ranches I used to serve—kept a roof over my head. When my dad died, I quit. Sold the house and moved back here to help my mom."

He opened his mouth and then suddenly shut it again.

Intrigued, she unfolded her legs and sat forward. "What were you going to say?"

"Nothing," he answered, reaching for another cookie from the plate on the coffee table.

"You were going to say something and stopped." She frowned. There was more to this story, wasn't there? Something he didn't want to talk about. Something about coming home.

"You're nosy, you know that?"

She grinned. "I'm a woman. We don't let anything drop."

"You're telling me." He sighed. "Look, let's just say I wasn't a big fan of my mother buying the diner. Running a small business is tough and she's worked hard her whole life. She's over fifty now and working harder than ever."

"You wished she had stuck with working her shift and going home at the end of the day. Leaving the stress behind."

"Yes."

She understood. He'd felt terrible when his own business had failed. He'd seen the bad reaction from people when his dad had failed. He wanted to spare his mother any or all of that. She got it. She even admired him for his protective streak.

"Some people aren't satisfied with that, Rhys. I wasn't. I wanted to build something. I wanted to know I'd done it and done it on my own. But I understand where you're coming from. I'm responsible for my employees, too. It's a big responsibility, not just financially but morally. At least for most people, I think, and if not it should be. People need to look at their employees like people and not numbers. Even if I wanted to make a change, I know I'm not the only one to consider."

"You thinking of changing?"

The question stirred something uncomfortable inside her. "Nah, not really. Like I said—I'm just overdue for a break, that's all."

She liked it better when they were talking about him. She put her hand on his knee. "You help her a lot, don't you? Around the diner. Fixing things and whatever needs to be done."

He looked away. "Of course I do."

"And you don't get paid."

He hesitated. "I'm not on the payroll, no," he said.

"You're a good man, Rhys."

She meant it. The things he said made perfect sense and only served to complicate her thoughts even more. She was enjoying the downtime too much. She hadn't truly loved the work for a while now, and she was finally admitting it to herself. Sometimes it felt pointless and frivolous, but every time she considered saying it out loud, she heard her father's voice proclaiming that very thing. She was just stubborn enough to not let him be right. Damn the Shepard pride.

Every time she thought about making a change, she was plagued by the realization that it wasn't just her who would be affected. Her employees needed wages. Her landlord was counting on her rent. Suppliers, caterers… All of that would trickle down, wouldn't it? Walking away would be just about the most selfish thing she could do.

They were quiet for a few minutes, until Rhys finally spoke up. "This business of yours, you've had to fight hard for respect, haven't you?"

"I'm sorry?"

"With your family. Your father's hugely successful, Jack's running what can only be considered an empire and Callum, while way more low-key, has fulfilled the family requirement for a spouse and grandchild. Must be hard standing next to that yardstick."

"I'm doing just fine, thank you." Indignation burned its way to her stomach, making it clench. She wanted to be able to tell him he was dead wrong. Problem was she couldn't.

"Hey, you don't have to tell me that. You're one of the most capable women I've ever met. But seeing your family at the rehearsal dinner, I got the feeling that you had to work just a little bit harder for the same recognition."

"You're a guy. You're not supposed to notice stuff like that."

She put her cup down on the table and folded her hands in her lap.

His voice was low and intimate as he replied, "I only noticed because I can't seem to take my eyes off you whenever you're around."

And there it was. The acknowledgment of whatever this was. Attraction. Curiosity. Carnality.

"I thought we weren't going to do this," she said softly. She kept her hands folded tightly in her lap to keep them from going where they wanted to go—on him. "I'm only here for a few days."

"Then there's no danger. We both know what's what. We're going in with our eyes wide open."

She looked up at him and was caught in his hot, magnetic gaze.

"Since that night in my truck, I can't stop thinking about you," he murmured, reaching out and tucking a piece of hair behind her ear. "I've tried. God knows I've tried." His fingers grazed her cheek and before she could reconsider, she leaned into the touch, the feel of his rough, strong hand against the sensitive skin of her face.

"Are you seducing me, Rhys?" His thumb toyed with her lower lip and her eyes drifted closed.

"With any luck." He moved closer, leaning forward slightly so she began to recline against the cushions. "We're adults," he stated. "We're both wondering. It doesn't have to go any deeper than that."

Tentatively she lifted her hand and touched his face. "Usually I'm the confident one who goes after what she wants."

He smiled a little, his gaze dropping to her lips. "You don't want this? I could have sworn you did."

"I didn't say that," she whispered, sliding deeper into the cushions.

"That's what I thought." His voice was husky now, shivering along her nerve endings. He leaned closer until he was less than a breath away.

The first kiss was gentle, soft, a question. When she answered it his muscles relaxed beneath her hand and he pressed his mouth more firmly against hers. Her pulse quickened, her blood racing as he opened his mouth and invited something darker, more persuasive. His hand cupped her breast. Her fingers toyed with the buttons of his shirt. He sat up and stripped it off, leaving him in just a T-shirt. She expected him to reach for the hem of her sweater but instead he took it slow, braced himself over top of her and kissed her again. His lips slid along her jaw to her ear, making goose bumps pop out over her skin and a gasp escape her throat.

"I'm in no rush," he whispered just before he took her lips again, and they kissed, and kissed, and kissed until nothing else in the world existed.

Taylor's entire body hummed like a plucked string. Rhys felt so good, tasted so good, and it had been too long since she'd felt this close to anyone. Yearning and desire were overwhelming, and his leisurely approach had primed her nearly to the breaking point. The words asking him to stay were sitting on her lips when he softened his kiss, gently kissed the tip of her nose, and got up off the sofa.

She felt strangely cold and empty without his weight pressing upon her. Maybe he was going to hold out his hand and lead her down the hall, which would suit her just fine. If he could kiss like that, she would only imagine his lovemaking would be spectacular and…thorough. She swallowed roughly at the thought and got up, ready to take it to the next step.

Except he was reaching for his coat.

Her stomach dropped to her feet while heat rushed to her face. "What…? I mean where…?" She cleared her throat, crossed her arms around her middle, feeling suddenly awkward. "Did I do something wrong?"

He shoved his arms into the sleeves but wouldn't meet her gaze. "Not at all. It's just getting late. I should go."

She wasn't at all sure of herself but she lifted her chin and said the words on her mind anyway. "For a minute there it kind of looked like you weren't going to be leaving."

For a second his hand paused on the tab of the zipper and the air in the room was electric. But then he zipped his coat the rest of the way up. "I don't want to take things too fast, that's all."

Too fast? Good Lord, she was leaving in a matter of days and he was the one who'd said he couldn't stop thinking about her. She wasn't innocent. She knew where this sort of make-out session was headed. And he was putting on the brakes without so much as a warning? Just when she thought she understood him, he did something else that made her wonder who the heck he was.

"What happened to 'we're both grown-ups'?"

Now he had his boots on. One moment they were sprawled on the couch and the next he couldn't get out of there fast enough. What in heaven's name had she done wrong?

"Let me take a rain check, okay?"

This night was getting stranger by the minute. "Rhys?"

He took a step forward and pressed a kiss to her forehead. "It's fine, I promise. I'll see you tomorrow."

Right. Because he'd be here twice. Great.

Still dumbfounded, she heard him say, "Thanks for dinner." Before she could wrap her head around what was going on he was out the door and headed for his truck. He didn't even let it warm up, just got in, started it up and headed out the driveway to the road.

What had just happened?

In a daze she gathered up the cups and the plate of cookies and took them to the kitchen. She expended her pent-up energy by washing the dishes and tidying the supper mess, and then went back to the living room to turn off the Christmas lights, still reeling from his abrupt change of mood.

His cotton shirt was still lying on the floor in a crumpled heap. He'd been in such a hurry to leave he'd forgotten to pick it up. She lifted it from the floor and pressed it to her nose. It smelled of soap and man and aftershave, a spicy, masculine scent that, thanks to the evening's activities, now elicited a physical response in her. Want. Need. Desire.

She stared at it while she brushed her teeth and washed her face. And when she went to bed, she left the penguin pajamas on the chair and instead slid into Rhys's soft shirt.

Having the material whisper against her body was the closest she was going to get to Rhys. At least tonight!

But the week wasn't over yet. And she was pretty sure
he owed her an explanation.

Rather than drive into Edmonton to shop, Taylor decided
to explore the Cadence Creek stores for Christmas gifts.
After her conversation with Rhys about running a small
business, she felt the right thing to do was to buy local and
support the townspeople who made their livelihood here.
For Avery and Callum, she bought a beautiful evergreen
centerpiece for their table from Foothills Floral. The craft
store sold not just yarn but items on consignment, and she
bought Nell a gorgeous quilt in pink and blue with patch-
work bunnies in each square. The men were a little harder
to buy for, but she ended up being delighted at the silversmith, where she purchased both her father and Jack new
tie clips and cuff links, the intricate design a testament to
the artist's talents.

While she was browsing the handcrafted jewelry, a particular display caught her eye. Beautiful hammered and
sculpted silver pendants on sterling chains shone in the
morning sunlight. She picked one up, let the weight of it sit
on her fingers, a delicate horseshoe with tiny, precise holes
where nails would go. She smiled to herself, remembering
asking for a lucky horseshoe at the wedding and how Rhys
had informed her that a rabbit's foot got rubbed for luck.

He'd amused her, even then when she'd been her most
stressed.

She let the pendant go and moved on. She still had her
mother's gift to buy and then the groceries for Christmas
dinner.

At the drugstore she picked up a gift set of her mother's favorite scent, and hit the grocery store for the turkey

and vegetables needed for dinner, loading everything in the trunk of her car. She must have done okay, because the bags nearly filled it to capacity.

The last stop was the bakery, where she figured she could grab something sweet and Christmassy for the holiday dinner and maybe sit and have a coffee and a piece of cake or something.

Anything to avoid going to the Wagon Wheel. She was too afraid of running into Rhys, and she had no idea what to say to him. Sleep had been a long time coming last night. This morning he'd been by early to do the chores, and was already gone when she'd finally crawled out of bed.

The first thing she noticed as she went inside was the welcoming heat. Then it was the smells—rising bread and spices and chocolate and vanilla all mingled together. Browsing the display, she immediately decided on a rich stollen, her mouth watering at the sight of the sugar-dusted marzipan bread. She also ordered a traditional Christmas pudding which came with a container of sauce and instructions for adding brandy.

They were going to have a traditional Christmas dinner, with all of them together for the first time in as long as Taylor could remember.

She was just sitting down to a cup of salted caramel hot chocolate and a piece of cherry strudel when Angela Diamond came in, her cheeks flushed from the cold. She spotted Taylor right away and came over, chafing her hands together and smiling. "Well, hello! I didn't expect to meet you in here this morning."

"I thought I'd do a little shopping before the honeymooners get back. It's hungry work."

"Amen. I like to cook but my talents can't compare to the goodies in here. Do you mind?" She gestured to the chair across from Taylor.

"Of course not! I'd love the company."

Angela sat and took off her gloves. "God, it's cold. I wish a Chinook would blow through and warm things up a bit. What are you having? It looks good."

Taylor laughed. Angela was quite chipper this morning. "Hot chocolate and strudel."

"I'll be right back. I need something decadent."

Angela returned shortly with a cup of chocolate and a plate holding an enormous piece of carrot cake. "I'll tell you a secret," she confided, leaning forward. "Since Avery joined forces with Jean, the quality has gone way up. The specialty in here used to be bread and that's it. Now it's everything."

"I bought a Christmas pudding," Taylor admitted. "It's the first time we've all been together in a long time. I'm thinking turkey and stuffing and the whole works this Christmas." She took a sip of her hot chocolate.

"When are Callum and Avery back?"

"The afternoon of the twenty-third."

"And when do you head back to Vancouver?"

Taylor sighed. "Boxing Day."

Angela put a piece of cake on her fork. "Sounds to me like you're not too excited about it." She popped the cake in her mouth.

"I should be. I've got a ton of work to do and not much time to do it in. Big New Year's party happening. I've left most of the work to my assistant. She's very capable, thank goodness."

"You're not enjoying the project?"

Taylor brushed a flake of strudel pastry off her sweater. "I've been doing this for a while now. When I started, some of the unorthodox requests I got were exciting. And I really liked being creative and working under the gun. But lately—"

She broke off. She really *was* having doubts, wasn't she? And then there was the conversation with Rhys last night. How could she even flirt with the idea of walking away when so many people depended on her?

"Lately what?" Angela asked.

"I think I'm getting jaded or something. Most of the events seem so extravagant and pointless."

"You're looking to create something meaningful."

Taylor put down her mug. She'd never quite thought of it that way. "I suppose I am. This party on New Year's Eve? It's just some rock star throwing cash around and showing off, you know? And it'll be fun and probably make some entertainment news and then it'll be gone twenty-four hours later and no one will remember. Weeks of planning and thousands of dollars for what?" She sighed. "It lasts for a few hours and then it's gone like that." She snapped her fingers.

For a minute the women nibbled at their treats. Then Angela spoke up. "You don't have to give up the business to make a change. Maybe you just need to switch the focus."

"What do you mean?"

Angela shrugged easily, but Taylor knew a sharp mind at work when she saw one. Angela had single-handedly started her own foundation for helping battered women. She was no lightweight in the brains or in the work department, and Taylor knew it would be smart to pay attention to what Angela said.

"Say, for instance, there's a non-profit looking to hold a fund-raiser. The board of this foundation is pretty on the ball, but organizing social events is not where their strongest talent lies."

"You're talking about the Butterfly Foundation."

Angela smiled. "Well, yes, in a way. But we're small.

We wouldn't have enough work to keep you going. But there's the housing organization that helped build Stu Dickinson's home after they lost their things in a fire. And many others in any part of the country you choose. I think you'd be very good at it, Taylor."

The idea was interesting, and to Taylor's surprise she didn't dismiss it right away. That told her something.

Angela put down her fork. "Look, I was a social worker before I started Butterfly House and the foundation. I was good at my job but I was frustrated, too, especially as time went on. I'm still using much the same skill set, but I finally started doing something I'm really passionate about—helping abused women get back on their feet. Anyway, think about it. We're going to be planning something for later this spring. I'll give you first crack at the job if you want it. Get your feet wet."

"Thanks," Taylor replied, her mind spinning. "But I can't just up and walk away from what I've built, you know?" It certainly wasn't as easy as putting in two weeks' notice and going on her way.

"Of course." Angela checked her watch. "And I've got to go. I'm picking my son up from a play date in twenty minutes. But I'm really glad we ran into each other."

"Me, too."

Angela got up and slid her gloves back over her fingers. "And merry Christmas, Taylor. To you and your family, if I don't see you again."

"You, too. Say hi to Molly and Clara for me."

After Angela was gone, Taylor sat at the table, her hot chocolate forgotten. Angela had been so right. What was missing from Taylor's job was meaning. It was why she'd been so flustered about things not being perfect at the wedding—it had been important to her on a personal level.

Right now she did a job because she was paid good

money to do so. And she had enjoyed the challenges that went along with the position of being sought after. But at the end of the day, all she had left was the satisfaction of a challenge met. She hadn't given anything back. What Angela suggested, an event like that had the power to make ripples throughout communities, a difference in peoples' lives. It would matter; last longer than a single night. Wouldn't that be amazing?

And then Taylor thought of her staff, and her leases, and the fact that they, too, had lives, and bills to pay.

Maybe Rhys was on to something after all. Maybe working nine-to-five was way easier. He'd just learned his lesson faster than Taylor, that was all.

But then, he'd been forced to shut down his company. As Taylor stood and put on her coat again, she let out a long breath. She didn't have that worry. Her company was well into the black. And as long as they stayed there, she was sure she could find an answer.

CHAPTER NINE

RHYS HOVERED AT the door to the barn, wanting to go to the house, but hesitating just the same. He'd been an idiot last night. It had all been going great. He hadn't even minded talking about the past so much. Maybe Taylor was right. She was an outsider and completely impartial, and it made a difference. She certainly hadn't judged.

But it hadn't just been about talking. Oh, no. Every time he was around her the sensible, cautious part of his brain shut off. The physical attraction was so strong and sitting alone, in front of the tree, with the cozy lighting and the way her eyes shone and her hair smelled…

Yep. He was an idiot. There'd been no room for logic. Just justification for doing what he wanted rather than what was smart.

He'd been ready to take it to the next level when warning bells had gone off in his head. At first it was knowing that he was on the verge of losing control and pushing his advantage, which he made a practice of never doing. Taylor wasn't as ready as she thought she was. It was in the sweetness of her kiss, the tentative way she touched him, the vulnerable look in her eyes. And just like the horses he worked with, he knew she had to be sure. She needed to come to him.

Except she hadn't, not this morning. He'd hung around

for a while, hoping to see her at the window or door, but nothing, and he'd been due for work at Diamondback and couldn't stay forever. Now he'd finished the evening chores and the lights were glowing at the house and still there was no sign of her. His hasty exit had probably hurt her feelings, he realized.

But there'd been a second issue, too, and one equally if not more important. He'd known exactly where things were headed and abruptly realized he had absolutely no protection. He was a guy who was generally ready for any eventuality, and he should have had a clue after the way the passion had exploded between them while parked in his truck. But he hadn't. And if he'd let things go any further, he might have been very irresponsible. Might have lost his head and let his body override his brain. He wanted to think he wouldn't, but he wasn't exactly objective when it came to Taylor, for some reason.

So he'd pulled the pin and gotten out. And not exactly gracefully.

It wouldn't happen again. A condom packet was nestled in his back pocket. He'd driven out to the gas station on the highway to buy it, because this town was so damn small that it would be just his luck that he'd be spotted at the drugstore and the rumors would start.

He told himself that the condom was just a contingency plan. He could get in his truck and go back home, or…

Resolutely he left the barn and latched the door behind him, and with his heart beating madly, took long strides to the house. He made no secret of his approach, his boots thumping on the steps and he knocked firmly on the door. Whether this went further or ended, some decisions were going to be made right now. He had to stop thinking of her like some nervous, inexperienced filly, afraid of her own shadow. Taylor Shepard was the most self-assured, confident woman he'd ever met. She knew her own mind.

The door opened and anything he'd considered saying died on his lips.

She looked stunning. She'd left her hair down, the dark mass of it falling in waves past her shoulders. Her jeans hugged her hips and legs like a second skin and the red V-neck shirt was molded to her breasts, clinging to her ribs and giving her the most delicious curves he'd ever seen.

"It's about time you got here," she said softly, holding open the door.

He didn't need any other invitation. He stepped inside and, with his gaze locked with hers, kicked the door shut with his foot. She opened her lips to say something but he caught her around the waist and kissed her, erasing any words she might have uttered. When he needed to come up for air, he released her long enough to shed his jacket and boots.

"Hello to you, too," she said, her voice rich and seductive. "Not wasting any time, I see."

"I'm done wasting time. Aren't you?"

The moment paused as her gaze held his. "I think I am, yes."

It was all the encouragement he needed. As a saucy grin climbed her cheek, he chuckled. And then he reached out, threw her over his shoulder in a fireman carry and headed for the hallway as her laughter echoed off the walls.

It was still dark in the bedroom but Taylor's eyes had adjusted to it and she could see shadows cast by the moonlight streaming through the cracks in the blinds. The dark figure of the dresser, a small chair, a laundry basket.

Rhys, snuggled under the covers beside her, his hair flattened on one side where he'd rested against the pillow.

Her heart slammed against her ribs just looking at him. Not in her wildest dreams had she been prepared for last night. Any impression she'd had of him as…well, she supposed ordinary was as good a word as any…was completely false. He'd been an exciting lover, from the way he'd taken control and carried her to the bedroom, to how he'd managed to scatter their clothes in seconds, to how he'd expertly made love to her.

She swallowed thickly. It had been more than exciting. It had been much, much more. He'd been physical yet gentle, fun yet serious, and he'd made her feel things she'd never felt before in her life. She'd felt beautiful. Unstoppable. Completely satisfied. And in the end, rather than skedaddling home as she expected, he'd pulled up the covers and tucked her securely against him.

She'd felt cherished. More than she'd ever imagined, Rhys Bullock was turning out to be someone very, very amazing. Someone who might actually have the power to chase away some of the ghosts of the past.

His lashes flickered and his lips curved the tiniest bit. "You're staring at me, aren't you?"

Heat climbed her cheeks but she braced up on her elbow and rested her jaw on her hand. "Maybe."

"I can't blame you. I'm really quite handsome."

Her smile grew. Had she really ever thought him plain and unremarkable? There was a humor in the way he set his mouth, the way his eyes glowed that set him apart, wasn't there? And then there was his body. She'd had a good look at it now—all of it. There was nothing plain about Rhys.

"Your ego knows no bounds."

"I'm feeling really relaxed this morning." He opened his eyes. "Why do you suppose that is?"

She dropped her gaze for a moment. "Rhys..." she said shyly.

"Is it okay I stayed all night?"

Her gaze lifted. "Of course it is." She preferred it. Things had happened so quickly. They'd touched and combusted. At least by him staying she didn't get the feeling it was only about the sex.

Which was troubling because there really couldn't be anything more to it, could there?

His hand grazed her hip, sliding beneath the soft sheets. "It was good."

She smiled, bashful again because they were still naked beneath the covers. "Yeah, it was."

For a few minutes his hand lightly stroked and silence filled the room. Taylor wished she could abandon all her common sense and simply slide into his embrace again, but being impulsive wasn't really her way. Last night she'd waited for him. She'd wanted this. But now? It was how to go on from this moment that stopped her up.

"Listen, Rhys..."

"I know what you're going to say." His voice was husky-soft in the dark. "You're going to say there's only the weekend left and Callum and Avery will be back and you'll be going to Vancouver."

Nervousness crawled through her belly. "Yeah, I was going to say that."

"Since we're both aware of that, the way I see it we have one of two choices."

She couldn't help but smile the tiniest bit. Rhys was used to being in charge. Even now, he was taking control of the situation. When they'd first met it had grated on her last nerve. But now not so much. It was kind of endearing.

"Which are?" she asked.

"Well, I could get out of bed and get dressed and do the

chores and we could say that this is it. No sense going on with something that's going to end in a few days anyway."

"That sounds like a very sensible approach."

"Thank you."

She might have believed him, except his fingers started kneading the soft part of her hip. She swallowed, trying to keep from rolling into the caress. "And the second?"

"I'm glad you asked. The second option, of course, is that we enjoy this for however long it lasts and go our inevitable separate ways with the memory of the best Christmas ever."

"Not as sensible, but it sounds like a lot more fun."

"Great minds think alike."

The smile slid from her face as she turned serious, just for a moment. "Do you think it's possible to do that?" she whispered.

Dark eyes delved into hers. "I'm not ready to say goodbye yet. I don't see as we have much choice."

She slid closer to him until they were snuggled close together, skin to skin. She hadn't counted on someone like Rhys. She'd thought she'd come here, watch her brother get married, recharge, go back to her life. Instead she was…

She blinked, hoping he didn't notice the sudden moisture in her eyes. She would never say it out loud. Couldn't. But the truth was, she suspected she was falling in love. She recognized the rush. The fear. The exhilaration. Something like that only happened once in a while, and it had been a long, long time for Taylor. It wasn't just sex. She had real feelings for Rhys. Saying goodbye wasn't going to be easy.

"Can I ask you something?"

"Sure." He, too, braced up on an elbow, more awake now.

"Why did you leave so fast the other night?"

"Oh, that." He smiled, but it had a self-deprecating tilt to it that she thought was adorable. "Truth is, things were happening really fast. And you caught me unprepared."

That was it? Birth control? She suppressed a giggle, but a squeak came out anyway. "You could have just said that," she chided. "Instead of rushing out like you couldn't stand being near me another moment."

"Is that what you thought?" His head came off his hand. "Maybe."

He leaned forward and kissed her lightly. "Nothing could be further from the truth. If I was in a hurry, it was because I was in danger of not caring if I had a condom or not."

Her heart turned over. She wondered if he realized how much he truly tried to protect those around him.

"Now, as much as I'd like to repeat last night's performance, I've got cows that need to be milked," Rhys said quietly.

"And then what?" She lifted her chin and looked into his eyes. The dark light was turning grayer as the night melted into day, highlighting his features more clearly.

"It's Saturday. I'm not due at Diamondback. I'm not expected anywhere, as a matter of fact."

"Then come back in for breakfast," she invited. "I'll make something good."

"You got it." He slid out of bed and she watched as he pulled on jeans and a T-shirt. He turned and gave her a quick kiss. "Look, I'll be a while. Go back to sleep."

"Okay."

He was at the doorway when he turned and looked back at her. "You look good like that," he said softly, and disappeared around the corner while her heart gave a little flutter of pleasure.

They had the weekend. She rather suspected a weekend wouldn't be nearly enough.

After breakfast Rhys went back home to shower and grab fresh clothing. In his absence Taylor also showered and did her hair and put on fresh makeup. She vacuumed the rugs and tidied the kitchen and wondered if he'd bring his things to stay the night. When he arrived again midmorning, he carried a bag with him containing extra clothes and toiletries.

Seeing the black case brought things into rather clear perspective. Their intentions were obvious. There was no need for either of them to leave the house now.

After a rather pleasurable "welcome back" interlude, they spent the rest of the day together. Rhys helped Taylor wrap the presents she'd bought the day before, cutting tape, tying ribbon and sticking a red and gold bow on top of her head while making a lewd suggestion. She made soup and grilled cheese and the long awaited Chinook blew in, raising the temperature and softening the snow. They went outside and built a snowman, complete with stick arms, a carrot for a nose, and rocks for the eyes and mouth. That event turned into a snowball fight, which turned into a wrestling match, which ended with the two of them in a long, hot shower to ward off any damp chill.

He did chores. She made dinner. They curled up in front of the television to watch a broadcast of White Christmas while Rhys complained of actors feeling the need to sing everything and Taylor did a fair impression of the "Sisters" song. And when it was time, they went together to Taylor's room.

By Monday morning Taylor's nerves were shredded. The weekend had been nothing short of blissful but in a few hours Callum would be home and her time with Rhys would be over. There was no question in her mind—her feelings for Rhys were real.

But what hope did they have? He would never be happy living in a city like Vancouver, and she could tell by the way he spoke and how he'd acted since they'd met that he wanted to stay close to his mother to look after her. She realized now that his desire to hold a steady job rather than being the boss was all about taking care of his family. What she'd initially seen as complacency was actually selfless and noble. From what she could gather, his need to care for Martha was, in part, a way to make up for the instability in her past. He'd hold things together the way his father never had—no matter how well-intentioned.

Despite Angela's ideas, Taylor couldn't see any way to avoid going home either. She had commitments and responsibilities at *Exclusive!* This was nothing new. She just hadn't expected that even the thought of leaving him would cause the ache she was feeling in her chest right now.

"Hey," he said softly, coming up behind her. She was standing at the kitchen window, looking out over the fields. "You look like you're thinking hard."

"Just sad the weekend's over, that's all."

"Me, too."

She turned to embrace him and noticed his bag by the kitchen door. "You're leaving already?"

"It's Monday. I'm due back at Diamondback, remember? I should have been there an hour ago."

Right. His job. Time hadn't stood still, had it? "You're working today?"

"And tomorrow."

Emptiness opened up inside her. This was really it then. She might not even see him again before her flight out on the twenty-sixth.

"Rhys…"

"Don't," he said firmly. "We both knew what this was from the start."

Dread of losing him sparked a touch of anger. Was she so easy to forget? So easy to leave—again? "And you're okay with that? Just a couple of days of hokey pokey and see you later, it's been fun?"

He gripped her upper arms with strong fingers. "We weren't going to do this, remember?"

"Do what?"

"Get involved."

"I am involved. Up to my neck, as it happens."

"Taylor."

He let go and stepped back, his dark eyes clouded with confusion. He ran a hand through his hair. "I should never have come back. I should have left well enough alone."

"You didn't. We didn't. I don't know how to say goodbye gracefully, Rhys."

To her chagrin she realized tears were running down her face. She swiped them away quickly. "Dammit," she muttered.

He came closer, looked down at her with a tenderness in his eyes that nearly tore her apart. "Hey, we both knew it would come to this. My life's here. Yours is there. You have *Exclusive!* to run."

Yes, yes, the damn business. When had she started resenting it so much? Even a quick check of her email on her phone this morning had made her blood pressure spike. She couldn't ignore reality forever. Didn't mean it didn't stink, though.

"Thanks for the reminder." She stepped back, wished she had something to occupy her hands right now.

Rhys frowned. "Look, Taylor, we both know you're competitive and a bit of a perfectionist. I like those things about you. I really do. But I also know that the drive and determination that made you so successful is going to keep you in Vancouver until you set out to do what you've wanted to achieve."

"Even if what I'm doing isn't making me happy?"

It was the first time she'd come right out and said it.

His frown deepened. "The only person who can decide that is you. But I'll caution you right now. Letting go of that goal isn't easy. There are a lot of things to accept. And I'm not sure you'd be happy walking away."

"And if I did walk away, would you be here waiting?"

Alarm crossed his features. She had her answer before he ever opened his mouth, didn't she? Oh, she should have listened to what he'd said ages ago when they'd first kissed. She was different from local girls, and she was low risk because she wasn't staying. The idea of her not going was scaring him to death.

"Look, Taylor…"

"No, it's okay," she assured him. "You're right. This was what we agreed and I don't have any regrets." That, at least, was the truth. She didn't regret the last few days even if there were mixed feelings and a fair bit of hurt. They'd been magical when all was said and done. And Rhys Bullock would be a nice memory, just like he said.

He came forward and tilted up her chin with his finger. "I know I'm where I belong. I learned my lessons, had my failures and successes. You're not there yet, that's all."

She pulled away, resenting his attitude. What did he know? She had her own failures, but she was glad now that she'd kept the baring of her soul to one messed up wedding and not the disaster that was her last relationship. "You're leaving anyway, Rhys. I'd appreciate it if you weren't patronizing."

The air in the room changed. There was a finality to

it that had been absent only moments before. Rhys went to the doorway and picked up his bag. Silently he went to the door and pulled on his boots and jacket. When he was ready he looked up and met her eyes. "I don't want to leave it this way," he said bleakly. "With us angry at each other."

"I'm not angry," she said quietly. "I'm hurting, and the longer you stay, the worse it is."

He stepped forward and pulled her into his arms for one last hug. "Hurting you is the last thing I wanted to do," he murmured in her ear. "So I'll go." He kissed the tip of her ear. "Take care, Taylor."

She swallowed against the lump of tears and willed herself to stay dry-eyed. "You, too, Rhys. And Merry Christmas."

He nodded and slipped out the door. The milder temperatures of the Chinook had dipped slightly and she could see his breath in the air as he jogged down the steps and to his truck.

She shut the door, resisting the opportunity to give him one last wave.

They'd set the ground rules. Leaving was supposed to be easy. It definitely was not supposed to hurt this much.

CHAPTER TEN

CALLUM AND AVERY arrived back home, happy and tired from their trip and with tons of pictures from Hawaii. Taylor found herself bathing Nell after dinner while Callum checked on the stock and Avery started to make a dent in the mountain of laundry from their luggage. When Taylor suggested she go back to the B&B for the next few nights, Avery insisted she stay. "The couch pulls out. Please, stay. I've missed having a sister around."

Taylor had no good argument against that so at bedtime the cushions came off the sofa and the mattress pulled out. Avery brought sheets from the linen closet. "Sorry it's not as comfortable as our bed," she apologized.

A lump formed in Taylor's throat. Memories she wished she could forget crowded her mind, images of the last few nights spent in the master bedroom. This morning she'd stripped the bed and put the sheets in the washer. Rhys's scent had risen from the hot water and she'd had to go for a tissue.

"Taylor, are you okay?"

"Fine," she replied. "Hand me that comforter, will you?"

Avery handed it over while putting a pillowcase on a fat pillow. "Callum said Rhys did fine with the stock. Did you see him much while he was here?"

Taylor met Avery's innocently curious gaze, watched

as her expression changed in reaction to Taylor's. "What's wrong? Did something happen with Rhys?"

Taylor focused on tucking the bedding around the mattress. "Of course not."

"Taylor." Avery said it with such meaning that Taylor stopped and sat down on the bed.

Avery came over and sat beside her. "I saw you dancing at the reception. And Callum said Jack said something to him about you and Rhys kissing in his truck the night of the rehearsal. There's something going on between you, isn't there?"

"Not anymore," she replied firmly. She wondered if she sounded convincing.

Callum came through to the kitchen carrying an empty baby bottle. "Hey, what's going on?"

Avery looked up at him. "Girl talk. No boys allowed."

Taylor saw her brother's expression as he looked down at his wife. He was utterly smitten. Having someone look at her that way hadn't been so important even a month ago. Now it made her feel like she was missing out on something.

"Who am I to get in the way of my two favorite girls?" he asked, then looked down at the bottle with a stupidly soft expression. "Well, two of my three favorites anyway."

Callum knew where he belonged. He was contented, just like Rhys. So why was it so hard for her to figure out?

"I'll leave you ladies alone, then. Gotta be up early anyway."

When he disappeared back around the corner, Avery patted Taylor's arm. "Wait here," she commanded, and she skipped off to the kitchen. She returned moments later carrying two glasses of wine. "Here," she said, handing one to Taylor. "Sit up here, get under the blanket and then tell me how you managed to fall in love with Rhys Bullock within a week."

"How did you know?" Taylor asked miserably.

Avery laughed. "Honey, it's written all over your face. And as an old married woman, I demand to know all the details." She patted the mattress. "Now spill."

Christmas Eve arrived, along with Callum and Taylor's parents and Jack, back from Montana bearing presents and a strained expression. His trip hadn't gone all that well, as the manager for his corporate retreat business had been in an accident, leaving no one to run things at his Montana property. He was going to have to go back down there right after Christmas instead of taking the break he'd planned.

But nothing kept Jack down for long, and as they all gathered in Callum's small house laughter rang out in the rooms.

"I wish we had room for everyone here," Avery mourned.

"The bed and breakfast is lovely, don't you worry," Susan assured her. "And Harry and I have a surprise for you. We're taking you all out for Christmas Eve dinner."

A strange sort of uneasiness settled in Taylor's stomach. Please let her say it was out of town and not at the diner…

Susan went on happily. "You two just got back from your honeymoon and you're hosting us all tomorrow for Christmas. Tonight someone else is going to worry about the cooking. It's all arranged. Martha Bullock is doing up a prime rib for us and then we'll go to the Christmas Eve service."

Oh, God. The Wagon Wheel? Really?

Taylor pasted a smile on her face. "Surely the diner closes early on Christmas Eve?"

Harry shrugged. "Mrs. Bullock said it would be no trouble, especially for just the six of us."

Avery caught sight of Taylor's face and jumped in. "What a lovely thought. But really, we can have something here. There's no need…"

"Are you kidding?" Jack interrupted. "Prime rib? I've been living on sandwiches for a week. I'm so there."

Avery looked over at Taylor. What could she say? Besides, there was no guarantee that Rhys would be there. It was Christmas Eve after all.

She gave a short nod. "Sounds good to me," she answered, trying to inject some enthusiasm into her voice. This great Shepard family Christmas wasn't going to be brought down by her bad mood.

During the afternoon everyone brought out their presents and put them under the tree, which was a major source of frustration to Nell, who got sick of the word *no* as she crawled through the living room and pulled herself up on the chair next to the decorated spruce. She went down for an afternoon nap and everyone relaxed with a fresh batch of one of Avery's latest creations—eggnog cupcakes—and hot spiced cider. It was supposed to be perfect. Magical. And instead Taylor could only think about two things— the work waiting for her back in Vancouver, and how much she missed Rhys.

Jack pulled up a footstool and sat beside her, bringing his mug with him. "You're awfully quiet today. What's going on?"

She shrugged. "Too long away from the city, I guess."

He nodded. "Can I ask you something?"

"Sure." Jack and Taylor were the most alike in her opinion. He tended to see the big picture in much the same way that she did. And they were the ones still single now, too.

"Are you happy, sis?"

The question surprised her. "What do you mean?"

He raised an eyebrow. "I recognize the look on your face."

Oh, Lord. If he guessed about Rhys she was going to wish for the floor to open up and swallow her.

"I saw it when I first got here, when you were planning the wedding," he continued. "How's business?"

"Booming," she replied.

"And how do you feel about that?"

She met his gaze. "What do you mean?"

Jack hesitated for a minute. "A few years ago, remember when the company expanded? New franchises opened up, and Shepard Sports launched south of the border. It was all very exciting, right?"

"Dad was ready to burst his buttons with pride."

"I wasn't. It was everything I'd worked for and yet…do you know what ended up making me happiest?"

Curious now, she leaned forward. "What?"

"The property I bought in Montana. The corporate retreat and team-building business. The sporting goods, well they're like numbers on a page. Units in and out. Sure, we do some special work with schools and organizations and that sort of thing. But it's just selling. The team building stuff, though, it's about people. I like that. I like meeting different people and finding out more about them. I like seeing groups come in and leave with a totally different dynamic. They come in and push themselves in ways they don't expect, which was the very best thing I liked about competing."

"That's really cool, Jack."

"I know. And because of it, I can look at you and see that what you're doing isn't giving you that same buzz. Something's missing."

"I've been doing some thinking," she admitted. "But you know what it's like. The bigger you get the bigger the responsibility. You can't just pull up and abandon what's already there."

Jack nodded. "There's always a way. And anyway, you've got good people working for you. You've been gone quite a while and everything's run in your absence, hasn't it?"

It had. Sometimes a little too well. Even when trouble popped up, a quick email giving her assistant the green light to solve the problem was all it took.

"Just think about it," Jack said. "Responsibility or not, there's no sense doing something if you're not happy at it."

"Thanks," she answered, taking a drink of cider. She was glad he hadn't assumed her reticence was caused by a man. That would have been a whole other conversation. Then Avery called her to the kitchen to taste Susan's recipe for cranberry sauce and the afternoon passed quickly.

They arrived en masse at the Wagon Wheel at six on the dot. A sign on the door stated that Christmas hours went to 5:00 p.m. on the twenty-fourth and closed on Christmas Day and Boxing Day. Just as she thought, Martha had stayed open for their family and Taylor was a bit upset at her parents for requesting it. Martha had family of her own, probably had plans too.

Inside was toasty-warm and two tables were pushed together to make plenty of room for the six of them plus the high chair for Nell. Nell was dressed in soft red pants and a matching red velour top with tiny white snowflakes on it. After her nap she was energized, tapping a toy on the tray of the high chair and babbling at the blinking tree lights. Taylor was laughing at her antics when a movement in the kitchen caught her eye. It was Rhys, dressed in one of Martha's aprons, taking the roast out of the oven to rest.

He was here. Her stomach tangled into knots and her mouth felt dry. They hadn't seen each other or spoken since the morning they'd said goodbye. From the strained expression on his face, he wasn't too happy about tonight, either. As if he could sense her staring, he looked up and met her eyes across the restaurant. She looked away quickly, turning to answer a question of her mother's about the upcoming event her company was planning.

Martha brought them all glasses of iced water and placed a basket of hot rolls in the center of the table. That was followed by a fresh romaine salad with red onion, peppers and mandarins in a poppy seed dressing that was delicious. Rhys stayed in the kitchen, out of everyone's way. The fact that he seemed to be avoiding her stretched her nerves taut, and by the time the main course was served she was a wreck.

Martha had outdone herself. Glazed carrots, green beans with bacon, creamy mashed potatoes and puffy Yorkshire pudding and gravy complemented the roast, followed by a cranberry bread pudding and custard sauce. By the time the plates were cleared away, Taylor was stuffed to the top. Her father checked his watch. "Seven-fifteen. We'd better get going," he announced. "The church service starts in fifteen minutes."

Everyone got up to leave, reaching for coats and purses and gloves. Everyone but Taylor. They really didn't see, did they? She'd bet ten bucks that Martha and Rhys probably wanted to go to church, too. According to Callum, most of the community showed up at the local Christmas Eve services. And the Bullocks were going to be stuck here cleaning up the mess instead of enjoying their holiday.

"Taylor, aren't you coming?"

"I'll be along," she said lightly. "You go on without me."

Avery gave her a long look, then a secret thumbs-up. Taylor returned a small smile, but it was quickly gone once the Shepard crew hit the door.

She went back to the table and started clearing dessert plates and coffee cups.

Martha hustled out from the kitchen. "Oh, heavens, girl, don't you worry about that! You head on to church with your family."

"What about you? Aren't you planning to go to church?"

Martha looked so dumbfounded that Taylor knew she had guessed right. "If I help it'll get done faster and we can all make it."

"Bless your heart."

"Where's Rhys?" Taylor looked over Martha's shoulder into the kitchen.

"He just took a bag of trash to the Dumpster out back. I swear I don't know what I'd do without that boy. He always says we're in this together, but he's got his own job." She handed Taylor the bin of dirty dishes and briskly wiped off the tables. "It was more than enough that he invested in this place for me. He's supposed to be a silent partner, but not Rhys. He thinks he needs to take care of me."

Taylor nearly dropped the pan of dishes. Silent partner? But Rhys was so determined to stay away from owning a business. How many times had he gotten on her case about it? And this whole time he was part owner in the diner and just neglected to mention it?

For the briefest of moments, she was very, very angry at him. How dare he judge her? And maybe he hadn't exactly lied, but he hadn't been truthful, either.

She remembered pressing him for something he'd been going to say. Now she got the feeling he'd almost let his stake in the diner slip while they'd been talking, and caught himself just in time.

"Rhys is part owner of the diner?"

Martha looked confused. "He didn't tell you? I mean, he

doesn't say much about it, but I thought the two of you…" Her cheeks flushed. "Oh. I've put my foot in it."

Taylor shook her head. "Not at all. We're not…"

But she didn't know how to finish that sentence. They weren't together but they weren't *not* together, either.

"I'm sorry to hear that," Martha said quietly, putting her hand on Taylor's arm. "You've been real good for him these last few weeks. And I think he's been good for you, too. You smile more. Your cheeks have more color. If I'm wrong tell me to mind my own business."

"You're not exactly wrong."

"He's needed someone like you, Taylor. Not that he's said a word to me about it." Her lips twitched. "He's not exactly the confiding type. Bit like his father that way."

Taylor knew that Rhys probably wouldn't like that comparison.

"My husband had his faults, but he always meant well. And he loved his family. I wish you were staying around longer, Taylor. You're a good girl. Not afraid to work hard. And I can tell your family is important to you."

She was perilously close to getting overemotional now. "Thanks, Martha. That means a lot to me. And Rhys is a good man. I know that. I'm sorry things can't work out differently."

"Are you?"

She swallowed. "Yes. Yes, I am."

Martha smiled. "Well, never say never."

The back door to the kitchen slammed and he came back in. A light snowfall had begun and he shook a few flakes off his hair. Their gazes met again and she fought to school her features. She should be angrier that he hadn't been totally honest, but instead all she could think of was how he had said he didn't want his mom to own the place. He'd gone against his own instincts and wishes to make her happy, hadn't he? Did Martha realize what a personal sacrifice he'd had to make?

They couldn't get into this now, if for no other reason than Martha was there and she should talk to him about it in private.

She marched the dishes into the kitchen. "Should I put these in the dishwasher?"

"What are you still doing here?"

"Helping. I thought you and your mom might like to go to the service."

"Then maybe you shouldn't have requested a private dinner after we closed."

Guilt heated her cheeks at his condemning tone. "I didn't know about that until it was a done deal. Avery even suggested they do something at home but my parents insisted."

"Really? It kind of struck me as exactly the kind of thing you'd be comfortable asking for. You know, like when you're planning an event and you just 'make things happen.' Right?"

"Are you really that mad at me, Rhys?" She tried to muster up some annoyance, some justifiable anger, but all she felt was a weary sadness.

He shoved a cover on the roaster and placed it—none too gently—in the commercial fridge. "I don't know what I am. I know my mom is tired and was looking forward to a quiet Christmas Eve. Instead she ended up here after hours."

"None of the staff would stay?"

"She insisted they go home to their families. It's their holiday, too." His voice held a condemning edge that made her feel even worse.

He really was put out and honestly she didn't blame him.

She hurried to put the dishes in the dishwasher while Martha put the dining room back to rights. "So you helped."

"Of course I did."

Yes, of course he did, because this wasn't just Martha's diner but his, too. "I'm sorry, Rhys. My parents didn't think. What can I do now? Can we still make it to the church?"

"Run the dishwasher while I finish up these pots and pans. We'll be a little late, and not very well dressed, but we'll get there."

Martha bustled back into the kitchen, either too busy or simply oblivious to the tension between Rhys and Taylor. "My goodness, you're nearly done in here. Rhys, let's just leave the sweeping up and stuff until Boxing Day. It's always slower then anyway."

"If that's what you want."

Martha grinned. "Well, what I want is to get a good dose of Christmas carols and candlelight, followed by a double dose of rum in my eggnog."

Taylor laughed. "Get your coat while I start this up."

Martha disappeared into the office. Rhys frowned at Taylor. "Why did you stay? You could have gone on with your family and been there with time to spare."

She shrugged. "Because tonight isn't about just my family. There are other people to consider, too." She tilted her head to look at him. "Why didn't Martha just say no when my father asked?"

What little softening she'd glimpsed in his expression disappeared as his features hardened. "Your father offered a Christmas tip she couldn't refuse."

Taylor winced. Her dad, Jack, her—they were all used to getting what they wanted. It simply hadn't occurred to her father that Martha would say no. And it wasn't that he was mean or unfeeling. Of course he would consider it fair to properly compensate Martha for the inconvenience.

But she rather wished he hadn't inconvenienced the Bullocks at all. It would have been more thoughtful.

"I'm sorry, Rhys. Can we leave it at that and get your mom to the church?"

His gaze caught hers for a prolonged moment. In that small space of time she remembered what it was to hear him laugh, taste his kiss, feel his body against hers. It had happened so fast, and now here they were, as far apart as ever. Trying to keep from being hurt any more than they already were.

"You'd better get your coat. You can drive over with us."

She rushed to grab her coat and purse and by the time she was ready Rhys was warming up Martha's car and Martha was shutting off the lights to the diner and locking the door. The parking lot at the church was packed and inside wasn't any better; the only seats were on the two pews pushed against the back wall. Taylor spied her family, several rows up, but the pew was full from end to end. She squeezed in with the Bullocks, sitting on one side of Rhys while his mother sat on the other. As the congregation sang "The First Noel" she realized that while everyone here was dressed up in their best clothes, Rhys wore jeans and Martha wore her standard cotton pants and comfortable shoes from work.

It didn't seem fair.

They turned the pages of their hymnbook to "Once in Royal David's City." It was less familiar to Taylor, and Rhys held out the book so she could see the words better. Their fingers never touched, but there was something about holding the book together that healed the angry words of before. When they finally sat down, Taylor took advantage of the hushed scuffle. "I'm sorry," she said, leaning toward his ear. "I really am."

The minister began to speak and she heard the words "Let us pray," but she couldn't. Rhys was staring down into her eyes and she couldn't look away. Not now. She wanted to tell him how much she hated the way they'd left things. Wanted to ask him why he'd never told her the truth about the diner. Wanted to kiss him and know that she hadn't just imagined their connection. Instead she sat in a candlelit church that smelled of pine boughs and perfume, the fluid voice of the minister offering a prayer of thanks for the gift of Christmas, and wondered at the miracle that she'd managed to fall utterly and completely in love for the first time in her life.

Her lower lip quivered the tiniest bit and she looked away. What was done was done.

And then Rhys moved his hand, sliding it over to take hers, his fingers tangling with her fingers. Nothing had really changed, and there was a bittersweet pain in her heart as she acknowledged the truth of that. At least he wasn't angry at her anymore.

During the sermon Taylor looked around at the people gathered to celebrate the holiday. Her big brother cuddling a sleeping Nell in the crook of his arm. Her parents sat in between with Jack on the other side and Amy Wilson beside him—an odd surprise. There was the whole Diamond clan—Molly, Sam, Angela, Clara, Ty, the kids. Melissa Stone and her fiancé, Cooper Ford, sitting with two older couples she assumed were their parents. Many others she recognized as guests from the wedding. Business people, professionals, ranchers. Ordinary folks. This was real. This was life. Not the glammed-up high-paced craziness she was used to living in. Somehow, between Clara's sunny generosity, Angela's steady advice and Martha's ready acceptance she'd managed to become a part of this town instead of remaining on the fringes, where she usually made it a policy to stay.

She'd changed. And she couldn't find it within herself to be the least bit sorry.

As if she could sense her thoughts, Angela Diamond turned in her seat and caught Taylor's eye. She smiled and turned back around.

For the first time ever that she could remember, Taylor had no idea what to do next.

An usher brought around a box with tiny white candles in plastic holders. As the service ended, the choir started with the first verse of "Silent Night" as the minister went along and lit the first candle on the end of each pew. The congregation's voices joined in for the second verse as Rhys leaned over a little and let the flame from his candle ignite hers. Soon they were all standing with their candles, singing the last verse as the piano stopped playing and there was no sound but two hundred voices singing the age-old carol a cappella.

It was the most beautiful Christmas tradition Taylor had ever seen.

And when the song ended, everyone blew out their candles, the minister gave the benediction and a celebratory air took over the sanctuary.

In the midst of the confusion, Rhys leaned over. "Are you staying at the house or the B&B?"

"At the house." She waved at someone she only half recognized and smiled. "Callum and Avery insisted. I got the sofa bed."

Rhys's dark complexion took on a pinkish hue. She shouldn't have mentioned sleeping arrangements.

"Can I drive you home?"

"What about your mom?"

"I'll take her now and come back for you."

She wasn't at all sure what she wanted. She had no idea where things stood or even where she wanted them to stand. And yet they both seemed determined to play this out for as long as possible.

"I'll wait."

He gave her a quick nod and turned to Martha. The older woman had clearly decompressed during the service, and now she looked tired. It didn't look like Rhys was going to have much fight on his hands, getting her to leave.

There was a lot of socializing happening in the vestibule. Avery and Callum were working on getting Nell into her snowsuit without waking her up and the other three Shepards were putting on their coats and wishing a Merry Christmas to anyone who stopped by and offered a greeting. Susan saw Taylor and frowned. "You don't have your coat on! We're nearly ready to leave."

"I'll be along a little later."

"But you didn't bring your car."

Callum joined the group, a blurry-eyed, half-awake Nell fully dressed and snuggled into his shoulder. "We ready to go? Santa will be along soon."

"I was just telling Taylor to get her coat."

Taylor let out a breath and smiled brightly. "I've got a lift home, actually. No worries. You go on ahead."

"A lift home?"

"Rhys is going to drive me."

"I just saw him leave with his mother."

Taylor resisted the need to grit her teeth. "He's coming back."

Harry stepped in. "Rhys. He was one of Callum's groomsmen, right? Is there something going on there?"

Avery looked panicked on Taylor's behalf and Callum's brows were raised in brotherly interest but it was Jack, bless him, who stepped in, Amy Wilson hanging back just a bit, as if she was uncertain whether to join the group or not. "Hey, Dad, I've been meaning to ask you something about a new property I'm interested in buying."

The topic of a property investment was enough to lure her father away and Taylor relaxed. "Don't worry," she said to her mother. "We'll be right behind you."

"You've got your phone?"

Taylor laughed. "Of course."

"We'll see you in a bit, then." She hurried off in the direction of Jack and Harry. Avery came over and gave her a hug. "We're off, too. Good luck."

"Thanks."

As Avery and Callum walked away, Taylor heard Callum say, "Good luck? What do you know about this, wife?"

The vestibule thinned out until there were just a handful of people left. Jack got their parents on their way and came back for Amy, offering her a lift home. They'd just turned out of the lot when Taylor saw Rhys pull back into the yard in his truck.

Her boots squeaked in the snow as she crossed the parking lot, opened the door and hopped up inside the cab. She wasn't sure what to say now, so silence spun around them as he put the truck in Drive and headed out of the parking lot.

"I'm sorry I was so hard on your family." He finally spoke when they hit the outskirts of town.

"Don't be. You were right. About a lot of things."

"Such as?"

"Such as this is exactly something I probably would have done. Like you said, I make things happen. That's my job."

"I shouldn't have said that, either."

She chuckled then. "Boy, we can even turn an apology into an argument. We're good."

He laughed, too, but it didn't do much to lighten the atmosphere in the truck.

"So you're really going day after tomorrow."

"Yeah."

More silence.

It was only a short drive to the farm. Taylor longed to ask him about the diner but didn't want to get in another argument and she sensed it would be a sensitive subject. Besides, what did it truly matter now? It really didn't change anything.

The damnedest thing was that she did want something to change. And she couldn't figure out what or how. She just knew it felt wrong. Wrong to leave here. Wrong to say goodbye.

"You've got a couple days off from Diamondback?"

"Yeah," he answered. "Actually Sam suggested we all take Friday off, too, so I don't actually have to be back to work until Monday. I thought I'd sneak Mom to Edmonton one of those days, let her take in some of the Boxing Week sales."

"You're good to your mom, Rhys. She appreciates you, you know."

"Someone has to look out for her. She's my mom. She doesn't have anyone else."

It made even more sense now, knowing he had a stake in the Wagon Wheel. "You're very protective of the people you care about."

"Is that a bad thing?" He slid his gaze from the road for a moment.

"On the contrary. It's one of the things I l…like most about you."

Yeah, she'd almost said "love." She took a deep breath.

This would be a stupid time to get overly emotional, wouldn't it?

They turned onto Callum's road. "The thing is, Taylor…"

"What?"

He frowned. "You're competent. Everyone can see that. You're confident and successful and clearly you know how to run a business. I don't know why you feel you have to prove yourself. Why you have this chip on your shoulder."

"Sometimes I ask myself the same thing, Rhys." She turned in her seat. "Remember the time you said that most guys were intimidated by smart women? You had something there. There's a lot I don't know and more I'm not good at, but I'm not stupid. I've never understood why I should hide that fact just because I'm a woman."

"So you push yourself."

"Yeah. I guess if this trip has shown me anything, though, it's that I don't need to try so much. That…" She swallowed, hard. "That there are things more important that I've maybe been missing out on. In the past I haven't paid enough attention to personal relationships." She sighed. "I've made my share of screw-ups."

"Figuring that out is a good thing, right?"

"To be honest, it's been a little bit painful."

They pulled into Callum's driveway. Rhys parked at the far side, giving them a little space away from the house, and killed the lights.

"Sometimes the best lessons we learn are the ones that hurt the most."

She laughed a little. "Helpful."

But he reached over and took her gloved hand in his. "I mean it, Taylor. My mother told me once that we rarely learn anything from our successes, and the best teachers are our failures. It hurts, but I have to believe it always comes out better on the other side." He squeezed her fingers. "I wish you didn't have to go."

She wanted to say "me, too," but it would only make things worse, wouldn't it? Why wish for something that wasn't going to happen?

"Right. Well. Before you go in…I uh…" He cleared his throat. "I saw this earlier in the week and…"

He reached into his pocket and held out a small rectangular box. "Merry Christmas."

"You got me a present?"

"It's not much."

"Rhys, I…"

"Don't open it now, okay? Let's just say good-night and Merry Christmas."

She tucked the package into her purse. "Merry Christmas," she whispered, unbuckling her seat belt.

She looked up into his face. How had she ever thought it wasn't handsome? It was strong and fair and full of integrity and sometimes a healthy sense of humor. Before she could change her mind she pushed against the seat with one hand, just enough to raise her a few inches so she could touch her lips to his. The kiss was soft, lingering, beautiful and sad. It was the goodbye they should have had yesterday morning. It filled her heart and broke it in two all at the same time.

"Goodbye, Rhys."

She slid out of the truck before she could change her mind. Took one step to the house and then another. Heard the truck engine rev behind her, the creak and groan of the snow beneath the tires as Rhys turned around and drove away for the last time.

She took a few seconds on the porch to collect herself. She didn't want her family to see her cry or ask prying questions. She had to keep it together. Celebrate the holiday the way she'd intended—with them all together and happy. And if she had to fake it a little bit, she would. Because she was starting to realize that she'd been faking happiness for quite a while now.

She was just in time to kiss Nell good-night; to sit with her family and share stories of holidays gone by. Jack arrived and added to the merriment. After her brother and parents left for the B&B, she stayed up a little longer and chatted with Callum and Avery before the two of them went down the hall hand in hand. No one had asked about Rhys, almost as if they'd made a pact to spare her the interrogation. But as she finally burrowed beneath the covers on the sofa bed, she let the emptiness in. Because in the end she was alone. At Christmas. And her heart was across town, with Rhys.

CHAPTER ELEVEN

CHRISTMAS MORNING DAWNED cool and sunny. Taylor heard Callum sneak out just after five to do the milking; she fell back to sleep until Avery got up and put on coffee around seven. With Nell being too young to understand it all, there was no scramble for presents under the tree. Nell slept late after the busy night before, and Avery brought Taylor a coffee then slipped beneath the covers with her own mug.

Taylor looked over at her sister in law. "I think I would have liked having a sister if this is what it's like. Jack and Callum's idea of this would be to count to three and jump on the bed and see if they could make me yell. Extra points if they left bruises."

Avery smiled. "It was like this for me and my sister. I'm really glad you're here, Taylor. It's been so very nice."

"I'm glad I came, too."

"Even though it's bothering you to leave Rhys?"

Taylor nodded.

They sipped for a moment more before Avery took the plunge. "Did you fall in love with him? Or was it just a fling?"

Taylor curled her hands around the mug. "It would be easier to say it was a fling."

"But it wasn't?"

She shook her head.

Avery laughed. "I don't know whether to offer my congratulations or my sympathy."

"What do you mean?" Taylor looked over at her. "Do I look happy about it?"

"Yes. And no. You light up when you talk about him, you know."

No, she hadn't known. Damn.

"Falling in love is a bit of a miracle, don't you think? So that's the congrats part. And the sympathy comes in because I can tell you're confused and that's not easy."

"I live in Vancouver."

Avery nodded. "When I met Callum, I lived in Ontario. My life and job were there."

"But you could quit your job. It's different when you own your own venture. It would be harder for you now, with your bakery business, wouldn't it?"

"Difficult, but not impossible."

Taylor let out a frustrated sigh. "Avery, I get what you're saying. I do. But I've spent years building this business and my reputation. I've known Rhys less than a month."

Avery smiled softly. "I know. If you didn't have the business in the way, what would you do?"

See where it leads.

The answer popped into her mind with absolute ease. But it wasn't just up to her. "Rhys never once asked me to stay or hinted at anything past our…"

"Affair?"

Taylor blushed.

Avery finished her coffee. "It's that serious, then."

"Look," she said, frustration in her voice. "Last night he said he wished I didn't have to go but that's not the same thing as asking me to stay or when I'm coming back."

"Why would he ask when he's sure of the answer? Have

you given him any reason to think you would stay? Told him how you feel?"

She hadn't.

"Only because I'm positive nothing could come of it except our being hurt even more. Besides, there's a good chance he doesn't feel the same way. He told me straight out that he liked me because I was a challenge. That I was low risk because I was leaving anyway."

Avery snorted. "Oh, my God, that's romantic."

Taylor couldn't help it. She started laughing, too. "I'll be fine, Avery, promise. I just need to get back to a normal schedule. And first we have a Christmas breakfast to cook. You're the whiz, but I'm happy to be your sous-chef today."

"Deal," Avery said.

Babbling sounded from the second bedroom and Avery grinned. "Let me get the princess changed and fed first."

While she was gone and the house was quiet, Taylor snuck out of bed and got the box from her coat pocket. She didn't want to open it when anyone else was around. Sitting on the bed in her pajamas, she carefully untied the ribbon and unwrapped the red foil paper.

Inside the box was a necklace—the very same horseshoe necklace she'd been admiring at the silversmith's the other day. She lifted it gently and watched the U-shaped pendant sway as it dangled from the chain. How had he known it was just what she liked? It was simple but beautiful. When she went to put it back in the box, she heard a strange ruffle when her fingers touched the cotton padding. Curious, she moved it out of the box and saw the folded note hidden beneath.

For all the times you need a horseshoe to rub for good luck. Merry Christmas, Rhys.

He remembered, but he'd hidden the note, as if he didn't want her to find it right away. As if—perhaps—he'd meant her to discover it after she was home again and it would remind her of the time they'd spent together.

She didn't know whether to laugh or cry.

She tucked the necklace back in the box. She wouldn't wear it today, not when everyone was around. She didn't want any more questions about her relationship with Rhys. She just wanted to keep this one thing private, like a secret they shared. Cherished.

But she thought about it as the rest of the family arrived, breakfast was served, presents were opened. And when there was a lull, she took the necklace out of her bag and tucked it into her pocket, where it rested warmly within the cotton.

An hour or so before dinner, it all got to be too much so she excused herself and bundled up for a short walk and some fresh air to clear her head. She was partway down the lane when a dull thud echoed on the breeze. She turned around to see her dad coming down the steps, dressed in Callum's barn coat and a warm toque and gloves. "Hey, wait up," he called.

She had no choice but to wait.

When he reached her they continued walking, the sun on the snow glittering so brightly that Taylor wished she'd put on her sunglasses. "It's been a good day," Harry said easily, falling into step.

"We haven't all been together like this in a long time." Taylor let out a big breath. "It's been good."

"Yes, it has."

Silence fell, slightly awkward.

"Taylor, I've gotten the impression you're not completely happy. Are you okay?"

Her heart clubbed. "What gave you that idea?"

"Your mother pointed out a few things. And then

there's this Rhys guy. You seem half miserable, half thrilled about it."

She huffed out a laugh. "That about sums it up."

"Is it just this guy? Or is it work, too?"

She frowned. "You don't have to sound so hopeful about it. I know you don't like what I do and you'd love to see me settled with kids like Callum."

There. She'd come right out and said it.

Harry let out a long sigh. "I haven't been very fair. Or put things the right way."

Her feet stopped moving, as if they had a mind of their own. "What?"

She looked up at him, suddenly realizing why his eyes seemed so familiar. They looked like hers.

"I don't hate what you do. I resent it a bit, that's all."

"I don't get it."

Harry started walking again. "Callum joined the military instead of going to college. It wasn't my first choice, but when your son says he wants to serve his country, it's a hard thing to find fault with. Then with Jack…we both knew he couldn't ski forever. But after his accident and after the scandal…" There was a telling pause. "When he came to me asking to help him start Shepard Sports, I couldn't say no. It was good to see the light in his eye again. He could have died on that hill."

"What does this have to do with me, Dad?"

"I built my company from the ground up, Taylor. Neither of my boys were interested in finance. But you… you weren't just my last chance to pass it on to one of my kids. I could see the talent in you. You're good at making money, maybe even better than Jack. And you weren't interested in the least in the market or fund management or anything I do."

"You wanted me to work for you?"

"With me. Eventually."

"I thought you thought what I do is stupid."

He stopped walking again. "I was jealous of it."

"You never said anything."

"I kept hoping you'd come to me. I didn't want to pressure you."

"Instead you just made me feel like a disappointment." She wasn't holding anything back today. Maybe Rhys's way of plain speaking was rubbing off.

"I know. And I'm sorry. The truth is that you should do what makes you happy. I can't put my wishes on you kids. I'm proud of all of you for being strong and smart enough to make your own way."

"Even if it's planning frivolous parties?"

He chuckled. "I've seen your mother work her magic enough times at our small functions to know that a big event takes massive planning. You've got a talent, Taylor. And again, I'm sorry that my selfish pride took away from that."

They turned around and headed back, the house waiting for them at the end of the lane, snowbanks curling along the driveway and the remnants of her snowman listing lazily to one side. Her father's approval meant a lot. But she was also realizing that his validation wasn't everything. Her restlessness and drive wasn't about proving herself. It was about looking for something that was missing. It was about meaning, not accomplishment.

"I wish I could tell you that I could join the firm, but I need something that makes me excited to get up in the morning, Dad. I know fund management isn't it. I'm sorry, too. I wish you'd told me sooner."

"All I've ever really wanted for my kids is for them to be happy. If you're not, I want to know if there's anything we can do to help."

"Oh, Daddy." She stopped and gave him a hug, warmth spreading through her as he put his strong arms around her and hugged her back. "Thank you for that. I've got to figure it out on my own, that's all."

"Well, anything worth having is going to take a lot of work. If it was easy it wouldn't mean half so much. And none of my kids are quitters."

"No, we're not."

"You'll figure it out," he assured her. "Now, let's get back. I'm getting cold and I swear I can smell the turkey clear out here."

Taylor walked beside her father, feeling like a weight had been lifted. And yet a heaviness remained, too. Because their conversation hadn't offered any insight into what she should do about her current situation. So much for her creative, problem-solving mind. All she could see right now was a massive New Year's party that needed finalizing and about a dozen employees who were counting on her to keep their lives afloat. Where could she and Rhys possibly fit into that?

No stormy weather or mechanical failures had the grace to delay her flight, so bright and early on Boxing Day Taylor took the rental car back to the depot and walked into the departures area of the airport. Her feet were heavy and her stomach felt lined with lead as she tugged her suitcases behind her. She should be glad to be going home to her apartment, her regular routine, familiar things. Her muffin and coffee from the café around the corner each morning. Walks in Stanley Park. Warmer temperatures. Shopping. Work.

It would be good. It would be fine.

After she checked her bags she went through security and to the gate, even though she had nearly an hour to spare. She checked her phone, going through the email that was waiting for her attention. There was a rather frantic one from her New Year's client, and Taylor's blood pressure took a sudden spike. It was only five days to the party and the construction of the aquariums was delayed. He'd emailed her on Christmas Day, for heaven's sake. Like she could—or would—have done anything during that twenty-four hour period. People did celebrate holidays, she thought grumpily. Even workaholics.

Her fingers paused over the keypad. Was that what she was? A workaholic?

She scanned through the rest, knowing she should cool off before responding, and saw an urgent reply from her assistant, Alicia. Everything was under control. The aquariums were set to be delivered on the morning of the thirtieth, the fish would come a day later when the tank conditions were at the proper levels, and everything else was on schedule.

Taylor let out a breath. Why had she even worried? Alicia could handle anything their clients dished out. She never panicked and she was incredibly resourceful. Heck, Taylor wasn't even really needed.

She put the phone down on her lap as the thought sunk in.

She wasn't really needed.

The truth should have been obvious before. She was great at her job. She knew how to make the impossible happen. It stood to follow that she'd train her staff the same way. Alicia had been her right-hand girl for three years. She'd managed smaller events on her own. This party was probably the biggest challenge they'd had in a while and all Taylor had done was been available by email simply to confirm or approve changes in plan. Alicia had done the grunt work. She and her team had put it together.

And yet Taylor couldn't just walk away. She owned the business after all.

Suddenly her conversations with family came back with disturbing clarity. *What you're doing isn't giving you that same buzz,* Jack had said. *Something's missing.* And he'd gone on to say that what had given him the most fulfillment was his corporate retreat business. That it was more than just buying and selling. That it was about people.

An even bigger surprise was how her father had taken her aside yesterday afternoon. Just before they'd gone inside, he'd added one little addendum to their conversation. "I want you to know that I couldn't have done what I have all these years without your mother. Without all of you. Don't let life pass you by, sweetheart. Build your business with people you trust, but build your life with people you love."

People you trust. People you love.

The solution was so clear she couldn't believe it had taken her so long to put it together.

Even though it was still a statutory holiday, she scanned through her directory and found the number she was looking for. A quick call later and she was heading to the gate desk where two service agents had just arrived.

"I need you to pull my bags, please," she said, holding out her boarding pass.

The first agent came to the desk. "I'm sorry? This is the flight to Vancouver, leaving in forty minutes."

"Yes, and I checked in and this is my seat, 12F. But I'm not going to be leaving on it, so I need you to pull my bags."

"Miss." She checked the boarding pass. "Miss Shepard. We're going to be boarding in about fifteen minutes."

"I'm not going to be on it." She tried to stay calm and

smiling. "And if I'm not on it, you're going to have to pull the bags anyway, right?"

"Yes, but…"

"I don't even care if I take them with me now. I can come back to get them. I don't care if my ticket can't be re-funded." Her smile widened even as the agent's expression grew more confused. She leaned forward. "Would it help if I told you I fell in love and decided I can't leave after all?"

The confused look morphed into sentimental amuse-ment. "You're absolutely sure you're not boarding this flight?"

"I've never been more sure of anything in my life."

"It might take a while. You'll have to pick them up at baggage services." She sent Taylor a wink. "I'll call down."

"Thank you! I'm sorry for the trouble. And Merry Christmas!"

"Merry Christmas," the agent returned, picking up the phone. "And good luck."

CHAPTER TWELVE

Rhys put the broom back in the storage closet and began running hot water for the mop bucket. He'd left Martha in bed with a cold; she'd insisted on getting up and coming with him to give the diner a good cleaning but he'd convinced her to stay in bed since she'd be needed when they opened tomorrow. Knowing she'd likely change her mind, he'd made sure to give her a good dose of cold medicine. She'd be asleep for a good few hours, getting some much deserved rest. He could mop the floors and do up the bank deposit without any trouble.

If only he could stop thinking about Taylor as easily. That last kiss she'd given him had been so sweet—a bit shy and a bit sad. He knew he had no choice but to let her go, but it was killing him. She'd awakened something in him that was unexpected and he didn't know how to make it go back to sleep. At least a dozen times in the past thirty-six hours he'd grabbed his car keys, ready to drive over to Callum's and tell her he wasn't ready to let what they had end. But he'd put the keys back on the hook every time. It already hurt to let her go. To prolong it would only make it worse.

Something made him shut off the water, a persistent thump that came from out in the main part of the restaurant. Frowning, he stuck his head out of the kitchen and called out, "We're closed!"

He'd nearly pulled his head back in when he saw the red boots.

His heart gave an almighty *whomp*.

She was supposed to be gone. Her flight was supposed to have left almost an hour ago. Maybe he'd been mistaken about the boots?

He slowly stepped through the kitchen door and into the front of the diner. There was no question, they were red boots. The only red boots like them he'd ever seen in Cadence Creek. Most of her body was hidden by the gigantic pine wreath hanging on the door, but he saw her long legs and the tails of her soft black and red coat.

He smiled as she knocked again, harder.

"Rhys, I know you're in there. Your truck is parked right outside."

His smile widened. God, he loved it when she got all impatient and bossy.

"I said we're closed."

There was a moment of silence. Then her voice came again, mocking. "Don't be an ass. Open the door."

He rather thought he could play this game all day. Except he did really want to see her. And find out why she was still here.

"Rhys!" she commanded. "It's freezing out here!"

He couldn't help it, he burst out laughing, half in surprise and half in relief that he actually got to see her again. He went forward and turned the lock back. Gave the door a shove and then there she was, standing in the snow, her dark hair in the customary braid and her eyes snapping at him from beneath a black hat, one of those stylish things women wore in the winter that wouldn't ruin their hair.

"Hello, Taylor."

She stepped inside, reached up and swiped the hat from her head and shoved it in her pocket. "Hi."

"I thought you were leaving today."

"I was."

He locked the door again and faced her, his pulse leaping as he registered the fact that she'd used past tense. "Wait. Was?"

She nodded.

"Your flight get canceled or something?"

"Nope."

"I don't understand."

For several seconds Taylor remained silent. "Do you have any coffee on or anything?" she asked. "I'm freezing."

She was stalling, and the only reason she'd do that was that she was nervous. "I put a pot on when I got here. Have a seat."

She went to one of the lunch counter stools and perched on it. He added the right amounts of cream and sugar to her cup and handed it over. "It's probably not as good as mom's."

"Where is she, by the way?"

"Home in bed with a cold."

"Oh, I'm sorry to hear that." Her face seemed to relax a bit, though—was she glad they were alone? He was still confused as hell. She was insistent on coming in but now that she was here, trying to get anything out of her was about like working with a pigheaded colt who refused to be bridled. Trying on the patience. Once he got the bit in her mouth she'd be just fine, he realized. It was just figuring out what to use to lure her in, make her explain.

"You're probably wondering why I'm here," she said softly, looking up at him with wide eyes.

Feelings rushed through him as he held her gaze. Pain, because prolonging the inevitable was torture of a special kind and they'd done it twice now. Hope, because for some reason she was here and not crossing thirty thousand feet over the Rockies. And tenderness, because he knew now that beneath the dynamo that was Taylor Shepard was one of the most caring, generous people he'd ever met. At the very least he could admit to himself that he'd fallen for her. Hard.

"The thought crossed my mind," he replied.

"I forgot to give you your Christmas present," she said, reaching into her handbag. "I apologize for the poor wrapping job."

She held out a thin plastic bag that bore the logo of one of the airport gift shops.

Amused, he reached inside and pulled out a key chain with a fuzzy fake rabbit's foot on the end.

"Someone told me that you rub a rabbit's foot for good luck." Her voice was barely above a whisper.

It was then he noticed the horseshoe hanging around her neck, just visible in the "V" of her coat and sweater. She was wearing his Christmas present. That pleased him more than it probably should.

"Do you think I'm in need of some good luck?"

She put down her coffee cup but not before he noticed her hand was trembling the slightest bit. She was nervous. So was he. He had no idea what this all meant but he got the feeling they were standing on the edge of something momentous. Somewhere he'd never wanted to be again. Until now.

"Why don't you try rubbing it and find out?" she suggested.

He felt like a fool, but she was here, wasn't she? He'd indulge her. He rubbed the tiny faux-fur foot.

"Ok, Luck," he said when he was done, spreading his arms wide. "Here I am."

She got up from the stool, went around the counter, and grabbed onto his shirt, just above where he'd fastened the last button. "And here I am," she whispered as she tilted up her head and kissed him.

His arms came around her by sheer instinct, pulling her against his body into the places where she fit so well. There was relief in holding her in his arms again, passion that ignited between them every time they touched. She tasted good and he kissed her back, loving the feel of her soft lips against his, the sleek texture of her mouth, the way she made the tiniest sound of pleasure when he nibbled on her lower lip.

"You're right," he murmured. "It *is* lucky."

She smiled against his lips, but then pulled away a little and simply rested in his arms, her head nestled in the space between his shoulder and neck. A lump formed in his throat. Whatever he'd said over the last few weeks, he'd been a liar. There was nothing easy or casual or temporary about his feelings for her. They were very, very real. It wasn't all physical. The way they were embracing now was much, much more than that. What a mess.

"Why didn't you tell me about the diner?" Her voice was slightly muffled against his shirt but he heard her just the same. It was not what he expected her to say.

"What?"

She pushed back out of his arms and met his gaze. "This place. Why didn't you tell me you were part owner?"

Nothing she could have said would have surprised him more. "Who told you that?"

"Your mother. Though I don't think she meant to. It slipped out the other night."

"It's not a big deal."

"It's a very big deal." She frowned, a cute little wrinkle forming between her eyebrows. "For all your talk about not wanting to own your own business, not wanting to be the boss. Heck, you even said you hadn't wanted your mother to buy this place."

"I really didn't want her to buy it. But she was determined. Once my mother gets something in her head…"

"Sounds like someone else I know. And you invested because?"

He frowned. "If I hadn't invested all the money I'd gotten for my house in Rocky, she would have mortgaged herself to the eyeballs to have it. As it is, this place is free and clear in another four years."

"You did it to protect her."

"Of course I did. I couldn't stop her from taking the risk, but at least I could help cushion the fall."

"You did it thinking that you'd never see your money back."

He remembered the heated discussions he'd had with his mother about taking such a big step. In the end he'd had no choice. Money was just money. This was his mother and Rhys knew he had to look out for her. "I did it knowing that was a very real possibility, yes. And not because I didn't think she could do it. I just know from painful experience how many small businesses fail. She'd already lost enough over her lifetime. Her whole nest egg went into buying it, plus Dad's life insurance money. If the diner went under, she'd lose everything."

Taylor must think him an idiot. He'd made a business decision for reasons that had very little to do with business.

"You did it for your mother."

"I know it was foolish. But she's my mom."

"And the job at Diamondback?"

"Security. The best way to take care of her, to protect her, was to minimize financial risk. At least I bring in a regular paycheck that I, or rather we, can rely on."

Taylor reached out and pressed her hand to the wall of his chest. "You are a dying breed, Rhys Bullock. You protect the people you love no matter what. There's nothing foolish about that. What about your brother?"

"He's been gone too long, I think. He's off doing his own thing. He just said, 'Whatever she wants.'"

It had been Rhys who'd come home and helped his mom through those first days of grieving. Who'd met with lawyers and bankers. There had been no way he was going to let her go through that alone.

Taylor squeezed his hands. "Let me guess, Martha insists on you taking your share of the profits."

"Of course. I draw out the same percentage of profit as I initially invested."

He didn't quite like the keen way she was looking up at him. Like she could see right through him. He wasn't exactly lying...

She lifted one eyebrow. "You use the profits to pay down the loan, don't you?"

Busted. "Perhaps."

"And your house?"

He met her gaze. If she was after the whole picture, she might as well have it. She could probably still catch another flight today.

"Rented." Because by using all his equity he'd had nothing left for a down payment.

"And Martha doesn't know. She thinks you own it?"

He nodded. "That's right. You're looking at a full-time ranch hand with a rented house, truck payment and not a scrap in savings."

"So that's why you didn't tell me? Pride?"

She was here. Things were bigger between them than he'd ever planned. "No, not just pride. There's more. You know I never wanted to be like my dad. I was so determined that I'd do better. That no one would suffer because of my mismanagement."

"But someone did?"

He nodded. "Her name was Sherry. She had a couple of kids. She was my office manager—and my girlfriend."

"Oh, Rhys."

"I let them down so completely," he explained. "She blamed me, too. For losing the business. For putting her out of a job when she had the children to support. For…" He cleared his throat. "For breaking her heart."

"So you carried that around, on top of losing the business?"

"She depended on me. I can't blame her for being angry." He ran a hand over his hair and looked in her eyes, feeling miserable. "So you see I don't have a lot to offer in the way of brilliant prospects."

She took his hand. "That's not true! You work hard and you put the ones you love first. You made your mom's dream come true. You're strong and honest and loyal. You've got two strong hands and the biggest heart of anyone I've ever met." Her smile widened. "Know what else you've got?"

"What?"

"Your ace in the hole. Me."

Taylor gazed up at him, filled with admiration for the man he'd become. He really had no clue, did he? Rhys was self-assured, knew his place in the world. But he didn't understand how extraordinary he was.

"You? Come on, Taylor," he said, pulling away a little. "Look at you. You're successful. Your business is profitable enough to keep you in designer boots and who knows what else. We're as different as night from day."

"Not as different as you think. Just so happens that

we're peas in a pod, you and me. I was in a relationship a while ago, too. At the same time as that wedding story I told you about—remember the bride with the allergy? I was so upset about that. I mean disproportionately freaked out. John accused me of being cold. Of caring more about the business than I did about our relationship. The thing is he was right. And so your little digs about proving myself really hit a nerve. I was at a crisis point and he bailed. You weren't the only one who thought you were incapable of making a personal relationship work, and I really wasn't interested in risking myself like that again, you know?"

"He was an idiot."

She smiled at Rhys's blind loyalty. "No, he was honest. And the truth is, I didn't invest enough in our relationship. Probably because I didn't love him. I loved the idea of him. But not him. The idea of losing him didn't make me lose sleep. It didn't break my heart or make this heavy pit of despair settle right here." She pressed her fist to her stomach. Her voice lowered to a whisper. "Not like it felt about an hour and a half ago while I sat in Edmonton airport wondering how I could ever be happy if I left you without telling you how I feel."

His lips dropped open. He hadn't been expecting that. Neither had she. Neither of them had expected any of this.

"Do you really think I care about your bank statement? Truly? When have I ever given the impression that my goals are about making money?"

He shook his head. "You haven't," he admitted. "It's always been about proving yourself, meeting challenges."

"That's right." She tugged on his hand. "Come sit down. I want to run something by you."

"Me? Why?"

"When we first met, you told me that a smart person knows their strengths, do you remember? My dad taught me that a smart person also sees the strengths in others. I want your honest to goodness opinion about something. Will you help?"

"Of course."

They sat side by side on the stools, swiveled so they were facing each other and their knees were nearly touching. Rhys wasn't just some ranch hand. He had a lifetime of experiences to draw upon and she trusted his judgment. "Do you think I could keep the event planning business in Vancouver going and branch out into something else that excites me personally? Can I do both?"

Possibility hummed in the air. Rhys sat up straight and tall. Neither of them were rushing through to the end of the conversation. They'd been through enough to know that what was said today was constructing the foundation of wherever they went from here. It deserved to be built with care and attention. "It depends. What are you thinking?"

"Angela put the idea into my head before Christmas. I mentioned that I'm getting tired of the here today, gone tomorrow scene. Remember when I was so stressed about the rehearsal dinner and you said it was because the event meant something personal to me? You were right. But you know what? The satisfaction from planning Callum's wedding was greater than I expected, too. She said what I want is to create something meaningful, and suggested I help plan an upcoming fund-raiser for the Butterfly Foundation."

"That's a great idea!" Rhys smiled at her. "The Diamonds have done a really great thing with that charity. I know they'd appreciate the help."

"What if I took it a step further and used my expertise to work for lots of charities and non-profits? I love what I do and I'd still have the challenge of that, but I think I'd feel like I was doing something important, too, you know?"

"How could you do that and still keep the Vancouver business going? You'd be spreading yourself pretty thin."

"By promoting my assistant. She can do it. She's handled this party on her own since I've been here and it's been one of the most challenging projects we've ever done. She's built her own team. I'd still own the company, and I'd still be involved, of course. But in a different way. Kind of like Jack is with his business. He's far more hands-on with his team-building stuff than with the sporting goods."

"Would you set up the new venture from the same office?" he asked. "It would cut down on expenses."

He hadn't put the two together. The two of them and the business change. "This might come as a surprise, but I was thinking about running it from here."

"From Cadence Creek?"

He sounded so surprised she faltered. Had she possibly misread the situation? "Well, yes. It's close to Edmonton, not that far to Calgary, and an easy flight to Vancouver or even Toronto. I have family here. And…" She looked down at her lap. She was so confident when it came to her work and capabilities, but when it was personal she wasn't nearly as sure of herself. John's words—*Incapable of what it takes to maintain a relationship*—still echoed in her head. Even though she didn't really believe them, they'd left their mark just the same. "I guess I thought you might like it if I were around."

"Taylor."

She couldn't read what emotion was in his voice other than surprise. Embarrassment flooded through her as she felt quite ridiculous. The old insecurity came rushing back. What if the problem was really her? What if she wasn't lovable? She'd spent so much time trying to be strong that it had become a shell around her heart.

"Of course, it's okay if you don't. I mean, we did agree

that this was a short-term thing, and I don't want you to feel pressured."

His hand touched hers as it sat in her lap. She stared at it for a long moment, watched as his fingers curled around hers, firm and sure. Her heart seemed to expand in her chest, filled with so much emotion she didn't know what to do with it all. She drew hope from the simple touch. Felt wonder at the newness and fragility of it all. And there was fear, fear that this couldn't all be real and that it would disappear at a moment's notice.

She put her other hand over his, tentatively, until she couldn't bear it any longer and she lifted their joined hands, pressing them to her cheek as her eyes closed, holding on to the moment as long as she could.

Rhys lifted his right hand, placed it gently along the slope of her jaw, his strong fingers whispering against the delicate skin there. "Taylor," he murmured, and she opened her eyes.

He was looking at her the way she'd never imagined any man would ever look at her. Wholly, completely, his lips turned up only the slightest bit, not in jest, but in what she could only think of as happiness. His eyes were warm, and looked on her with such an adoring expression she caught her breath. The pad of his thumb rubbed against her cheek, and he pulled his left hand from her grasp. He placed it along her other cheek, his hands cupping her face like a precious chalice, and he slid closer, so slowly it was sweet torture waiting for his lips to finally touch hers.

She thought the sweetest moment had to be in that breathless second when his mouth was only a fraction of an inch away, and all the possibilities in the world were compacted into that tiny space. But she was wrong. Sweeter still was the light touch of lips on lips, soft, tender and perfect.

"You're staying?" he asked, his voice barely a whisper in the quietness of the diner.

"I'm staying," she confirmed.

He pressed his forehead to hers and she slowly let out her breath as everything clicked into place.

"I tried not to fall in love with you." Rhys lifted his head, smiled, and patted his lap. She slid off the stool and onto his legs, and he put his arms around her, strong and secure.

"Me, too. I kept telling myself it was a fling. But I couldn't get you off my mind. You're bossy and you drive me crazy, but you're loyal and honorable and you…"

She broke off, feeling silly.

"I what?"

He gave her a jostle, prompting her to finish her sentence. "It's corny." She bit down on her lip.

"I don't care. What were you going to say?"

She leaned against his shoulder. "You make me feel treasured."

He tilted his head so it rested against hers. "And you make me feel invincible."

She smiled, the grin climbing her face until she chuckled. "I'm glad."

His smile faded as his face turned serious. "I won't let you down."

"You couldn't possibly."

He kissed her again, more demanding this time, and when he lifted his head her tidy braid was well and truly mussed. "Hey," she said, running her fingers through his hair. "Now that I'm going to be here on a permanent basis, we can take all the time we need to fall in love."

"Honey, I'm already there."

She smiled. "Me, too. But I want to enjoy being this way a little longer. Is that okay?"

"Look at me. I'm in no position to argue."

She kissed him again, thinking that she could happily stay that way forever when he gave her braid a tug.

"Hey," he said. "I know we're taking our time and all that, and I don't mean to rush, but what are you doing New Year's Eve? Do you have plans?"

She nodded slowly. "I do have plans, as a matter of fact."

"Oh." Disappointment clouded his voice.

"I think I'd like to spend it right here, in your arms. If that's okay with you."

"That's more than okay. And the night after that, and the night after that."

She snuggled closer. "I don't know what the future holds. Changes are coming, adjustments and transitions are going to be made. But I know one thing for sure. You're my anchor, Rhys. Somehow you make everything right simply by being. And for the first time, I don't have to have all the details sorted and everything planned to the last item. Things will fall into place. And do you know how I know?"

He shook his head.

"Because I didn't plan for you. And you were the best thing of all."

He kissed her hair. "I love you, Taylor."

"And I love you."

And that was all she really needed to know.

* * * * *

Look for all Donna Alward's future books in
Harlequin American Romance.
The CADENCE CREEK COWBOYS *series*
concludes with Jack and Amy's
story coming soon!

ROMANCE

Million Dollar Christmas Proposal	Lucy Monroe
A Dangerous Solace	Lucy Ellis
The Consequences of That Night	Jennie Lucas
Secrets of a Powerful Man	Chantelle Shaw
Never Gamble with a Caffarelli	Melanie Milburne
Visconti's Forgotten Heir	Elizabeth Power
A Touch of Temptation	Tara Pammi
A Scandal in the Headlines	Caitlin Crews
What the Bride Didn't Know	Kelly Hunter
Mistletoe Not Required	Anne Oliver
Proposal at the Lazy S Ranch	Patricia Thayer
A Little Bit of Holiday Magic	Melissa McClone
A Cadence Creek Christmas	Donna Alward
Marry Me under the Mistletoe	Rebecca Winters
His Until Midnight	Nikki Logan
The One She Was Warned About	Shoma Narayanan
Her Firefighter Under the Mistletoe	Scarlet Wilson
Christmas Eve Delivery	Connie Cox

MEDICAL

Gold Coast Angels: Bundle of Trouble	Fiona Lowe
Gold Coast Angels: How to Resist Temptation	Amy Andrews
Snowbound with Dr Delectable	Susan Carlisle
Her Real Family Christmas	Kate Hardy

Mills & Boon® Large Print
November 2013

ROMANCE

HISTORICAL

MEDICAL

1013 GEN STD LP

Mills & Boon® Hardback

December 2013

ROMANCE

Defiant in the Desert	Sharon Kendrick
Not Just the Boss's Plaything	Caitlin Crews
Rumours on the Red Carpet	Carole Mortimer
The Change in Di Navarra's Plan	Lynn Raye Harris
The Prince She Never Knew	Kate Hewitt
His Ultimate Prize	Maya Blake
More than a Convenient Marriage?	Dani Collins
A Hunger for the Forbidden	Maisey Yates
The Reunion Lie	Lucy King
The Most Expensive Night of Her Life	Amy Andrews
Second Chance with Her Soldier	Barbara Hannay
Snowed in with the Billionaire	Caroline Anderson
Christmas at the Castle	Marion Lennox
Snowflakes and Silver Linings	Cara Colter
Beware of the Boss	Leah Ashton
Too Much of a Good Thing?	Joss Wood
After the Christmas Party...	Janice Lynn
Date with a Surgeon Prince	Meredith Webber

MEDICAL

From Venice with Love	Alison Roberts
Christmas with Her Ex	Fiona McArthur
Her Mistletoe Wish	Lucy Clark
Once Upon a Christmas Night...	Annie Claydon

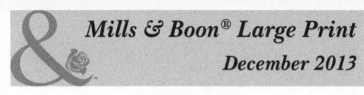

Mills & Boon® Large Print
December 2013

ROMANCE

HISTORICAL

MEDICAL